WHEN WORDS GET IN THE WAY

Rebecca works for a PR company organising the forthcoming centenary celebrations of Daniel Seymour's company. Although a successful businessman, Daniel struggles to accept that, as a divorcee, he has failed at marriage. Whilst Rebecca, after her parents' divorce, shies away from emotional commitment, not wanting history to repeat itself. Although from different worlds, they are both independent and wary. Will they move in the right direction — or be carried off-course by their own uncertainties?

√ VJ DC (M.E) MC H.P NWA
SZ

WENDY KREMER

WHEN WORDS GET IN THE WAY

Complete and Unabridged

LINFORD
Leicester

First published in Great Britain in 2009

First Linford Edition
published 2010

British Library CIP Data

Kremer, Wendy.
　When words get in the way. - -
　(Linford romance library)
　1. Businessmen- -Fiction. 2. Divorced
　men- -Fiction. 3. Public relations
　personnel- -Fiction. 4. Love stories.
　5. Large type books.
　I. Title II. Series
　823.9′2–dc22

　ISBN 978–1–44480–377–8

Published by
F. A. Thorpe (Publishing)
Anstey, Leicestershire

Set by Words & Graphics Ltd.
Anstey, Leicestershire
Printed and bound in Great Britain by
T. J. International Ltd., Padstow, Cornwall

1

'Rebecca you've no choice! I'm stuck here waiting for them to put my leg in plaster. You're my only hope.'

Rebecca Lomax looked at her alarm clock with drowsy eyes. Her brain was still half-frozen; it was half-past-six. 'You want me to take over? This morning? You must be joking Don!' She pushed herself to a sitting position and ran her neatly manicured fingers through her auburn hair.

'You wrote the text, so it's not completely foreign to you. You only need to get there on time, speak the right sentences at the right moment, and give them the prepared information folders. There's a first time for everything and there's no reason for you to panic! I'm sure you'll manage. Roger knows how to set up the technicalities; he's already done it for

1

me a couple of times.'

'Why not just phone when their office opens? When you tell them you've broken your leg in two places, they're bound to understand.'

There was an edge to Don's voice. 'If you do business with Seymour's, you don't ever 'postpone' anything, for any reason. I hope you realise I had to sweat blood to get this far.'

Rebecca's brain was gradually catching up, and apprehension was replacing lethargy. 'There there must be someone else. Send Tony or Fay. It's their area not mine, I'm the background worker, remember — the text writer.' Her voice was tinged with alarm at the prospect her boss was churning out for her.

'They went to Scotland yesterday; they're after the whisky distillery job, remember?'

She bit her lip. 'Oh, yes! I'd forgotten.'

'You see! Something like this is above Roger's present abilities; he's only been with us for three months. That leaves you, the freelancers, and Vera. Vera still hasn't sorted out who takes sugar in their coffee, and she's been with us five years! You don't honestly think she could cope, do you?'

There was a knot in her stomach and her green eyes were wide and worried. 'Oh Don! Please don't ask me! I'll make a fool of myself and let you down.' She clutched her cell phone like a lifebelt in a stormy sea.

His voice was friendlier. 'No you won't!' He added hastily. 'I won't blame you if things go wrong, promise! I can't turn you into a perfect presenter at such short notice, but it's more important to keep our word, than it is to lose the contract to someone else . . . Becky, I'm only asking you to do the best you can.'

Rebecca was silent. She was tumbling down a slope, and there was nothing to break her fall. Don had always been a decent boss, and they got on well.

He sensed he was gradually winning her round. 'Aw! Come on Becky, please! I know I'm asking a lot, but I'm depending on you.'

'Perhaps you'll be able to make it, after all?' She grabbed at the fragile hope; his answer smothered her last chance of escape.

'Not likely. They've just brought some injured people in from a serious road accident; they have priority over everything else. Even if things go faster than I anticipate, I'd have to turn up in blue and white striped pyjamas and my leg in plaster up to my backside! If I'm home by lunchtime, I'll be lucky. Next time I'm thirsty in the middle of the night, I swear I'll go back to sleep, instead of tripping over the cat in the dark.'

With her heart in her mouth she gave in. 'I don't seem to have any choice, do I? But don't blame me if it ends as a gigantic fiasco. Where are the details? And I hope to heaven that Roger really knows how to handle the player?'

Relieved to have finally persuaded her, Don replied quickly. 'Don't worry, he does. He already has the DVD presentation and has a written copy of my text as well. I rehearsed it with him yesterday. You'll see I've marked spots where I intended to add my comments in red, and there's a suitable pause in the presentation at those spots. Make a copy of Roger's version and use that. Tony and I made the presentation using Power Point and your text, so it'll be straightforward.'

Rebecca doubted it very much but didn't comment.

He continued firmly. 'By the time you get to the office, *you'll* have about an hour to sort yourself out. You'll have to leave by nine to make sure you get to Seymour's on time; take a taxi just to make sure there are no delays.'

She queried. 'What if someone asks questions during or after the show?'

'You'll have to waffle your way through. Tell them you haven't thought about that aspect and you'll look into it and let them know.'

Her brain was whizzing. 'Don, I need

to know about this company. What's the contract about? I can't remember writing text for Seymour even if you're telling me I did.'

'Probably because we gave you bits and pieces of it when you were already up to your neck in the Thompson Chemical contract. I don't think you had any time to do detailed investigation on Seymour at the time. You still produced good stuff though. There's a glossy flyer and newspaper cuttings about the company on my desk. Basically, they're celebrating the company's 150th Anniversary and want a platform to get some extra publicity. They want a PR company to handle it and deal with the ballyhoo for the press, to push magazine articles, to create a company brochure, and to rope in the local TV. They also want a venue for the company gala in three month's time. The information folders are ready; they're in the top left hand drawer of my desk; it's not locked. Put one in front of every chair before everyone arrives.'

Rebecca searched her brain, without success, for snippets on Seymour. She got out of bed, her toes searching blindly for her slippers, and headed for the bathroom while still talking to Don. 'What should I wear?'

'A costume or a trouser suit. Daniel Seymour is managing director, and if his secretary's clothes are anything to go by, he's conservative. I'd guess he doesn't go for anything garish or too bright.'

Rebecca's mind ruffled through her wardrobe. She had a navy trouser suit, worth all the money she'd paid for it because it looked good and emphasised her slim figure. With a white blouse, it would be perfect. She realised, with a sinking heart, she had to iron a blouse. That would take ten minutes off her time. She'd reached the shower unit. 'Can you put Roger in the picture? I need to go through the script before-hand.'

'I'll phone him straight away, and

only hope that he's at home, and not out on the tiles with a girlfriend. You've got my number?'

'Yes, sure do.'

'Well get along then! Good luck, and don't worry! I know it's asking a lot of you, but I can't think of another solution.'

'If I had more time, I'd figure out an answer to that.'

'Phone me later and let me know how it went.'

While she waited for Roger in the otherwise empty office, she studied the information on the Seymour Company, and its managing director. The man sounded interesting; a typical manager with the ability to be ruthless when it was necessary.

Even though he was always in line to take over the family concern, Daniel Seymour has built a remarkable career, starting at the bottom and working his way up. He stated: 'A good leader is someone who does what he says, and says what he does. It's all about bringing out the best qualities in me and in the company so that customers want to do business with us.' What makes a good leader? — Seymour's answer: 'The ability to achieve what you aim for — but you have to handle people properly or you're just heading for trouble. I treat my workers with respect, and I also think people recognise I treat them as equals. I don't try to walk around with a sign that says I am the manager. One thing I do very well is know when I need to be a manager and when I need to be a colleague. I hope people feel comfortable with me; but I never forget that I'm responsible for the company and I carry the can.' According to Seymour, one of the best and most valuable experiences of his life was his time spent in the Army. 'I learned a lot there.' he said. 'It was a great maturing ground. I learned about loyalty, trust and procedure.' It's clear that he also honed his leadership abilities.

Seymour is a divorcee, his ex-wife

was on board a small aircraft when it went down off the coast of West Australia four years ago. She was the super-model June Moreland. The marriage was on the rocks and officially over before the crash happened. There were no children. Seymour has not re-married, although he replied with tongue in cheek he was open to suitable offers. Recently he's been partnering Lucinda Martin a lot — she's heiress to the Martin cosmetic millions. He skilfully avoided commenting on their friendship.

She was already nervous before Roger arrived and it wouldn't get better. Roger was in his early twenties, his hair was usually dishevelled, he had a rangy body, and clothes that looked the wrong size. He tried to pretend he was a skilled veteran however hectic the situation got, but nervous eyes and moist hands gave him away. Becky liked him; he was a willing worker and a pleasant personality. They began to make a copy of Don's presentation.

Once a few pages were ready, Rebecca started to read through it. By the time Roger finished copying, it looked like a thick bundle but Becky knew that Don didn't like lengthy presentations, as he believed prospective customers got fed up and bored if it dragged on too long. Becky comforted herself with the thought that in fact it was only roughly fifteen minutes viewing time. The added comments she had to make were only sprinkled here and there. If she followed Don's written plan carefully, things might work. She wished that they'd time to rehearse it once before they left, but knew it was a better idea to be sure they had everything, and get there on time. Roger looked worried but she reassured him. She'd be in the firing line; no one would stare at him if things went wrong.

Rebecca shouldered her bag, and hoisted her briefcase. They sailed confidently through Seymour's entrance area and went towards the main reception desk. Their appointment was confirmed and they were directed to the sixth floor, room 608. She was still on edge, although outwardly she looked unruffled. She'd already mentally rehearsed her opening gambit in the taxi, and she went through it again in her mind as the lift whizzed upwards.

Room 608 was opulent. A dozen thickly upholstered office chairs were spread around a huge oval table of honey-coloured wood. The thick carpet deadened all sound as they walked in. They'd barely arrived when a smartly dressed middle-aged woman appeared, introduced herself as Mr Seymour's secretary and showed Roger where to find the controls for the hidden screen and the sockets for electricity. She glanced briefly at a side table where a plate of fresh sandwiches and vacuum coffee pots were standing. She didn't ask why some unknown woman was in charge of the presentation instead of Don Williams. She looked at her watch. 'They'll be here in ten minutes. Or do you need more time to set things up?'

12

Rebecca looked at Roger. He gave a positive signal. 'No, that's fine.'

His secretary was satisfied and went out again.

Becky wanted to get it over and done with as soon as possible. Roger fiddled with the technical connections, and she was relieved to find things worked when he did a brief trial run. She placed the folders with their company's logo in front of each chair as Don had told her to.

The sound of talking in the corridor heralded people's imminent arrival. Becky positioned herself at the end of the table next to Roger. He was waiting for her signal. The room filled with men in business suits. They divided themselves around the table. One man with a commanding air of self-confidence detached himself from the rest and came towards her extending his hand.

'Good Morning! Daniel Seymour. And you are?'

Becky got up, and shook his hand. 'Good Morning! I'm Rebecca Lomax, representing Don Williams.' He was tall with a wide-shouldered, rangy body. She looked up into an arresting pair of light grey eyes. As she let go of his warm hand, she had a quick impression of aesthetic good looks, a lithe physique, a dark tailored suit and a white shirt. Experience of lots of other businessmen she'd met in the course of her work, told her he was unquestionably someone who was in charge of it all.

He imperceptibly nodded and speaking with smooth confidence as he turned away, he said. 'Well, let's see what you have to offer Miss Lomax. Bob, lower the blinds please!'

Someone at the back hurried to oblige, and the room fell into semi-darkness.

2

Rebecca sat down again. The presentation hadn't even started yet and her opening gambit was superfluous because the boss already knew who she was. She couldn't read the text either because she was in semi-darkness.

She swallowed a lump in her throat and took the plunge. 'Can I have a spotlight, please?'

Someone accommodated, and a quick glance back revealed Daniel Seymour was sitting at the head of the table. His eyebrows were raised and his expression wasn't particularly encouraging either. Rebecca took a deep breath, and hoped for the best. She didn't try to keep in eye contact with anyone once she started. She knew it was more important to get the text right. 'Good Morning! Don Williams Public Relations would like to welcome you to our plans for your forthcoming 150th Anniversary Celebrations.' She nodded to Roger and he started the presentation.

The next twenty minutes were some of the longest in her life. She had to concentrate hard not to lose her place in the text while keeping half-an-eye on the screen. She stumbled over sentences once or twice, and her heart plunged. On the one hand she was glad that no one asked questions, but on the other she was worried, in case it was a counter-productive sign. The final scene faded and Rebecca spoke the closing lines that expressed the hope that their suggestions had met with approval. She thanked them for their attention, and assured them Don Williams would be pleased to make adjustments or come up with alternative suggestions if desired.

Rebecca's blouse was stuck to her back, and she was glad the jacket also camouflaged the perspiration under her arms. Someone opened the blinds and a murmur of voices preceded the rustle of paper as people picked up the folders with all the relevant information. The odd person nodded politely in her direction as they sauntered in loose groups towards the door. Daniel Seymour came towards her; his long fingers clutching his folder. He towered over her chair and leaned forward slightly in her direction.

There was a dubious expression on his face and he said with quiet emphasis. 'Excuse me asking, but in your career, have you often been in charge of a presentation, Miss Lomax?'

She got up and her chin was in a stubborn line as she faced him. There was no point in denying it, and she didn't have Don's permission to explain why she was here, so she just replied. 'No.' She waited, offering no other details.

He surveyed her carefully and registered the creamy skin, the shoulder length hair that bounced when she moved, and her green eyes flecked with gold that had more than a hint of defiance. 'Well, can you at least tell me why we should give the contract to your firm and not to someone else?'

She repeated what she'd often heard Don say. 'Because our proposals are what we honestly think would be right for you, because we never try to push our clients to accept something they dislike, because we don't charge exorbitant rates, and because we always do an excellent job.'

Daniel pushed his free hand deep into a pocket. His mind burned as he mused that this girl had exactly the same colour hair June had had once years ago, although June's had come out of a bottle, and this woman's was too natural to be anything but real. In the back of his mind he recalled memories of the last time he'd seen his ex-wife. It was the day they left the divorce court. June had walked out with half his fortune and a sneer on her face. The court settlement was still a thorn in his side. At that time June had been making more money in a week than he had in a month, but it didn't prevent her lawyers trying to bleed him dry. He was sure she'd only dragged things through the courts out of sheer spite. His lips thinned as the memories returned. Rebecca registered his cold expression and how his pale eyes looked like bits of stone. He came back to the present and nodded as he began to turn away. As an afterthought he said. 'Help yourself to coffee before you go. Good Morning!'

She still felt very tense as she watched him walk away with easy strides and replied, 'Thank you! Good morning Mr Seymour!'

He'd not given her an inkling of encouragement, but now he'd left the room Rebecca didn't really care. She waited until the door closed and flopped down into the nearest chair. Relief was plastered across her face. Roger grinned, gave her a thumbs-up sign, and went to pour hot coffee into pristine white cups.

Rebecca phoned Don as soon as they got back to the office.

'Hmm! It sounds like you got through it okay!'

'There's no reason to feel optimistic. I don't think you can fool Daniel Seymour. I think he knew I was just a stopgap.'

'You got through it without a real hitch, that's the main thing. If you came across as absolutely incompetent, Seymour would have left you high and dry. He's that kind of manager; no time for fools. He stayed to the end, that's definitely encouraging.'

Rebecca laughed softly. 'Then it was only because he thought your ideas were in line with his demands! How are you? Is your leg in plaster?'

'Yeah! I'm home again — there is nothing else important on my schedule. I'll use today to get used to getting about on my crutches, and to catch up on the paperwork in my briefcase.'

'Will you be in tomorrow?'

'Definitely! Doris will drive me in,

and pick me up every day. The only trouble is she passes an awful lot of clothes shops on the way, so I'm sure the next couple of weeks will see an increase in her already bulging wardrobe.'

★   ★   ★

That evening Rebecca met her boyfriend Ken. He was a journalist and often away on projects for his newspaper. Their relationship was comfortable; one of sporadic meetings whenever he was in town. They ordered food and Rebecca smiled at him. 'How did it work out? Did the editor tear it apart again, paragraph by paragraph?'

'No, this time he seemed to like most of it.'

Rebecca studied his pleasant features and ash-blond hair. She was fond of him, he was a thoroughly nice person, and they had a good relationship. Her mother had already branded him as future husband material. That irritated Rebecca, but she realised it was a normal reaction. She was nearly twenty-seven, and her mother hoped to see her married and settled down.

'This time he didn't quibble about its length, and he wants me to go to India for a series of articles about how the burden of the dowry system is leading to mass abortion of female babies.' He paused. 'I thought it'd be a great chance for us to visit Goa for a couple of weeks on holiday; before I start my research.'

Becky was taken by surprise by his news, and even more by his suggestion. 'India? That certainly is a real feather in your cap! Well done! When do they want you to start researching?'

'In about five weeks' time. Well, what do you think about Goa? It's a great tourist location. Perhaps we could take in the Tadsch Mahal in a stop-over?'

Going on holiday with Ken would put their relationship on a new footing, and instinctively she replied, 'It's a great idea but it's not feasible, I'm sorry to say.'

'Why not?' He demanded.

'My job! I can't get leave without decent notice. My desk is covered with things waiting for me to finish, and there are some new contracts on the horizon.'

He remarked stiffly. 'You're entitled to holidays, like everyone else.'

'Yes, but they'd need to juggle things around a lot, if I'm not there for a couple of weeks. I can't just go at the drop of a hat.'

Ken sighed and ran his fingers through his hair. 'It isn't working, is it?'

She was puzzled by his expression. 'What isn't?'

'Us! I hoped we had a serious relationship lined up for the future. Do you want us to go on meeting like this until we're both old and grey? Where are we going here? I thought you liked me?'

She tried to control her rising irritation. He was trying to corner her.

'I do like you. What's that got to do with India? I like my work and I don't intend to lose it, that's all.'

There was a moment's silence and he watched her with disappointed eyes. 'It's your ingrained independence and ambition, isn't it? You don't let anyone get too close. You won't commit yourself, because that would mean you'd have to change your well-ordered world.'

Rebecca felt under attack. 'And you? You give work top priority, so why can't you imagine that mine is just as important to me!' She looked at him and went on determinedly. 'I'm not afraid of commitment; the trouble is we are both motivated people. How can you even think about a serious relationship when you don't know where you'll be in two days time? And don't pretend you don't like your nomadic life because you do! I accept it, but don't expect me to organise my whole life around you. I didn't realise you were making any kind of plans for us for the future.'

He spoke as if he hadn't listened, ignoring her comments he said. 'Have you ever thought about the fact that you'll end up lonely if you're not prepared to commit yourself to a lasting relationship?'

She replied with more resolve in her voice than she felt. 'I'm not exactly in my dotage, and I will commit, if my feelings tell me it is right for me. If not, perhaps that's the price a woman pays to feel comfortable and keep her independence.'

'Don't you want to settle down? We all have to compromise.'

'Do we, Ken? You may not admit it but women usually have to compromise a lot more! My father left my mother for someone who was twenty years younger. My mother was too old to build a completely new life for herself when my brother and I were off her hands. I don't intend to end up in a similar position.'

'If you could listen to yourself, you'd

see how brittle that sounds. You know I'd do my best to support you, whatever you did. You can't shut life out. If the right person comes along, you'll have to throw caution to the wind. Just because your parent's marriage didn't work, well, that doesn't have to mean the same thing will happen to you.'

Rebecca was trying to control her growing annoyance. 'Let's not argue about it. I'm sure things will sort themselves out. But don't push me!'

He shook his head and got up quickly. His expression was sombre. Looking down at her he said. 'No, things won't change! Our relationship is heading nowhere, today, tomorrow or next year. You don't care for me, otherwise you'd react differently now.' He shrugged and looked tense. 'I really hope you find what you're looking for Becky, but clearly whatever it is, it's not with me.'

She couldn't believe this was happening. She'd been looking forward to a pleasant evening and it was turning into a bit of a nightmare. 'If that's how you feel!' She sounded more determined than she felt. 'I hope that you'll find someone who fits in with your ideas better than I do.' Tears were burning behind her eyes. Some niggling regrets wished he wasn't going — but deep down she knew he'd become a comfortable and undemanding habit. 'I'm sorry I can't be what you want me to be.'

'So am I! Good luck Becky. If you ever meet someone to fill your emotional needs, don't think twice about the whys and wherefores, if you go on ignoring your own instincts you'll end up unhappy, and I genuinely, sincerely hope you'll never be that.'

She watched him give the waiter some money before he left. He didn't look back as he hurried out the door. Rebecca waited for a few minutes, took a last sip of the rough red wine, and then went out determinedly into the emptiness of the dark street.

Home again, in her small flat, she

wasn't sleepy, and knew there was no point in trying to sleep. She curled up on the sofa and let her thoughts wander. She'd known Ken for almost half a year but she was sure she'd done the right thing not to pretend. She didn't love him; her feelings were too bland for that. She liked him a lot, but he was not her dream man. If such a man existed she was certain she'd be willing to put her own independence on slow-burn.

★   ★   ★

Weeks passed and work went on. Whenever she'd been busy on a particular project, the name of the company or person she'd been involved often caught her eye later on. One day she spotted a picture and a short paragraph in the gossip column of a national paper about Daniel Seymour accompanying Miss Lucinda Martin to a charity ball. Rebecca studied the picture carefully. The woman was sleek, blond, and extremely attractive. The way she was gazing up at him suggested plainly that Miss Martin was interested in more than a sedate waltz on the dance-floor.

One Tuesday morning Don hobbled out of his office still leaning on a crutch and with a wide smile splitting his features in two. His face was thin with a strong forehead and bushy grey brows that jutted out over his watery blue eyes. He stopped in front of Rebecca's desk. 'If it wasn't so painful, I'd be tempted to break my leg more often.'

Rebecca looked up at him puzzled. 'What do you mean?'

'I've just had a phone call from Seymour. We've got it!'

If someone had knocked her off the chair, she couldn't have been more surprised. 'They . . . they've picked us?'

Don was grinning from ear to ear. He was absolutely delighted. 'A real feather in our cap, and you did it! Seymour is a top notch company. Well done!'

'I don't believe it! Not after my performance!'

He replied quickly. 'You clearly weren't that bad. Perhaps the contents of the presentation convinced them.' He ran his hand over his chin thoughtfully and shrugged. 'Who cares? Thanks to you, our rivals are tearing their hair out by the roots at this moment.'

Comprehension set in and Rebecca smiled up at her boss but looked slightly puzzled. 'Strange! I had a feeling Daniel Seymour took a personal dislike to me; there was a strange expression on his face when he left after the show. He recognises a good firm though, even if I wasn't word perfect.'

Just a few days later, Seymour's said they wanted to talk to someone who would be in charge of writing the text. Rebecca was used to visiting clients, although it wasn't automatically part of her job. Sometimes Don sent her if he thought it would bring better results, and give her more insight into the company involved; other times it was easy find what she needed via the internet or other sources. This time she was feeling particularly nervous — because her appointment was with Daniel Seymour.

For her meeting, she chose something from her everyday wardrobe of good quality working clothes. Becky reasoned Daniel Seymour wouldn't notice what she was wearing as long as it was neat and tidy. He was only interested in her ability to do her job. She arrived in plenty of time and his secretary showed her to a small reception room next to her own office. 'Mr Seymour will see you in a couple of minutes.' She gestured to a vacuum jug and cups on a nearby cabinet. 'Help yourself to coffee.'

'Thanks!'

Irene Taylor's eyes viewed her closely. Usually Daniel delegated this kind of thing to someone else. What was going on?

'I'll come for you as soon as he's free.'

3

Rebecca hung her jacket in a niche and straightened her grey pencil skirt and pale green cashmere sweater. She'd dithered a while before she bought the sweater, because of the price, but in the end she had thrown caution to the wind, and was now glad she'd done so. It skimmed her breasts, hinted at her slim waist and generally gave her a marvellous feeling of luxury. She picked up one of the thick glossy magazines from the side table and started to flip through the pages. Today was like a visit to the doctors — she wanted to get it over quickly and she hoped it wouldn't be repeated for a long time again. She started to read an article about the Provence; her concentration was interrupted by the sounds of voices as Daniel Seymour escorted his previous visitor to the outer door. Rebecca listened to the murmur of voices as he spoke to his secretary, and then the door opened and he stood looking at her.

'Good morning Miss Lomax! I see that you aren't just a presenter, but that you're also busy in other areas too. Will you follow me?' Her eyes froze on his long, lean form. He turned and walked briskly away without waiting for a reply, expecting her to follow.

Rebecca rushed to comply, hurriedly depositing the magazine back on the table and hoisting her shoulder bag into position as she did so; she didn't have time to slip into her jacket again. He waited inside his office door politely and closed it behind her before he marched towards his desk. It was positioned in front of a glass wall with a panorama view of the city. He folded himself into the leather chair and gestured. 'Make yourself comfortable.' He pushed a bundle of papers to one side of the desk, and picked up a folder with Don's logo on the cover from a pile on the other. He opened the cover and flipped through the pages it contained.

Rebecca gazed at him with reluctant admiration. He was a good-looking man; she guessed he was in his mid-to-late thirties. He was tall; at least six foot. His dark brown hair was short and cut neatly; it tapered out just above the perfect collar of his business shirt. His smooth skin had a slight tan. His features were thin, the nose straight, the eyes an intriguing pale grey beneath well-shaped eyebrows. His mouth was generous, his chin square and determined. He was a man who knew where he was going, and how he was going to get there. Rebecca's scrutiny ended as he looked up and began to talk. She concentrated on what he was saying.

'I see that Don Williams has put you in sole charge of the text. Wouldn't it be more sensible to work with a second person? It might generate more ideas and produce unique structuring.'

Rebecca didn't flinch although her

mouth felt dry. 'I'm in charge because that's what I do in the company. There is no one else. If my boss had to pay for two text-writers, he'd have double the expense and that would add to your costs. He's completely satisfied with my work.'

'What makes you the right person for tackling this particular job?' His eyes were sharp and lingered on her face. He was watching her carefully and monitoring her reactions to his questioning. When he examined her, apart from the bronze, copper, and chestnut highlights in the shoulder length hair, he saw she didn't look a bit like June. Her hair matched the sea-green eyes and creamy skin to perfection. The faint sprinkling of freckles on the bridge of her nose and thick eyelashes framing the almond shaped eyes completed a very pleasing and interesting picture.

Rebecca straightened her shoulders and wished she didn't have the feeling that she was under a microscope. Their talk reminded her more of a job-interview than an exchange about what line of approach she should take to create publicity for his company. 'I think I have a pretty good feeling for people and what they want.'

An arched eyebrow indicated his surprise. 'Do you?' Promptly he asked. 'What do you think I want?'

Her green eyes met his grey ones, and a streak of determination asserted itself. 'Someone who understands enough about your world and the things you offer and sell, to present them advantageously to the rest of the world in a way you approve of.'

His light grey eyes, with their glinting hints of silver in their depths, were intently appraising. 'You seem to be ambitious! Not just for your company, but for yourself personally!'

He was forming a follow-up question before she'd properly answered the previous one. She said with quiet emphasis. 'Does it matter?' She couldn't understand where he was heading. 'Surely it's only important that I do my job well, for the sake of your company and mine. Personal ambition shouldn't govern how I get those results.'

The silver in his eyes flickered and he paused slightly before he spoke again. His voice sounded friendlier, but his question was still probing. 'Are you scared of me, Miss Lomax?'

Again his question surprised her, but she decided it was time to come out of the corner. If he was direct with her, she could be too. With heightened colour she replied tersely. 'Should I be? To be honest, I suspect that you enjoy intimidating people if it suits your purpose — especially if you want to put someone on their defences. No, you don't scare me, Mr Seymour. I'm here to do my job and find out if my company's ideas and yours run on the same tracks. If they don't I hope we can work together to find a compromise. I always try to do a first-rate job, and till now our customers have been happy with the results. Nothing else counts.

Not much good ever comes out of being scared of someone, even if that someone is in a powerful position. Cooperation and teamwork is productive, anxiety and fear is fruitless.'

Daniel looked at her, his interest was aroused. He liked women who knew their own minds. He leaned back. 'Good! I need honesty, because it generates a good working relationship and brings results.' He studied some papers from the folder. 'What do you intend to work on first.'

She felt the tension lessen; they were getting down to business at last. 'Don, Mr Williams, thought I ought to tackle a company brochure first — one for your main customers. As the company is 150 years old, I suggest it'd be interesting to do a short history with a couple of photos for them, and the more usual kind of glossy flyer for the rest.'

'Hmm! It depends on what it costs. Have you an idea of how many customers we have world-wide? How many pages?' His slim fingers picked up a gold barrelled fountain pen and began to play with it restlessly as they spoke.

'Eight perhaps? Printed in compact booklet form. I need to do some research about the company history first, and then I can come up with a prototype and rough cost estimation for you to approve or not. Is there a company archive by any chance?'

He studied the wide-set jade eyes, the fine high cheekbones, the soft mouth with a resolute set to it, and the supple young body. His brow wrinkled slightly. 'We have a lot of important business papers in store, but I presume that you want more of the company's personal history?'

Rebecca nodded. 'Business papers show how a company grew and developed, but I'd like to interweave the company's commercial successes with the family history and use a more personal approach whenever possible. We've found that the majority of people who go to the bother of reading PR stuff that lands on their desks will glance at booklets, but they tend to ignore anything plastered with diagrams and commercial hum-drum. In the long run the personal angle attracts the most attention and it will strengthen ties. Your company was, and still is, a family concern, with a family member still managing it. It's the perfect platform to generate the right kind of PR interest. Family ownership in this day and age is rare — and so in your case, we can use the private aspects to gain lots of professional interest.'

He nodded impassively. 'My father may be able to help you on that sort of thing; we haven't many private records in the companies anymore. He retired a couple of years ago, but he's always collected family papers, photos, and other relevant information. I'll have a word with him, perhaps you can take a look at what he has, and use some of that?' He closed the folder.

'That sounds like just the kind of information I need. In the meantime,

I'll analyse the company's commercial success via the normal channels. I expect there are lists of the goods and services you dealt in through the years?'

'Perhaps ... there are the usual delivery notes, records on transportation jobs, lists of things we bought and sold, company assets, that sort of thing. I'll ask my secretary to poke around and find out what may be of use.'

She nodded. 'If possible I'd also like to contact any former employees who worked during the war or times of crisis, because memories about those times always go down well.'

He stroked his chin. 'That's a long-shot these days. People who worked for us in wartime are pretty old now. The company headquarters has moved around several times, and there were, and are, production-sites all over the place, but I'll ask if the personnel department can help you locate anyone.' He made a swift note on a block and looked at his watch.

She took the hint and got to her feet.

'Seymour's started out as a haulage company didn't it?'

He stood up and came round the desk towards her. 'Yes, with one horse and ramshackle cart in a small country town.' He gave her a slow smile, and Rebecca thought how it completely changed his expression and made him look almost young — the stiffness and severity was gone. 'From there it expanded, and at some stage we started involving ourselves in manufacturing the products as well as transporting them.' They were now on the way to the door. 'We changed direction whenever the time and the situation necessitated. Today we have factories, production lines, chemical works, engineering services, and wholesale businesses, here and abroad. If one branch is having a hard time the others have to compensate.' He opened the door. 'I'll see what I can do about the family history, and I'll be in touch.'

He held out one hand and grasped the framework of the door with the other. Rebecca took it and shook hands. 'Thank you for your time Mr Seymour. I'll look forward to hearing from you.'

His eyes had a faint glint of amusement in them as he said. 'You're welcome!'

She turned away from him and, and went to retrieve her jacket. She guessed that Daniel Seymour was already busy with the next task on his agenda. She went on her way with more of a spring in her step than when she arrived.

★   ★   ★

Rebecca got lots of information about Seymour's from the usual sources she used, and various additional items from the company's archives. There was plenty to make the flyer, but not what she wanted for a commemorative booklet. Don sent Seymour's the mock-up flyer for approval. It was authorised and Rebecca went to pick up the end proofs for checking, before it was finally printed. Back at the office, she took off her coat and checked her incoming e-mails. There were a couple. One name caught her eye immediately — it was from Daniel Seymour. She hurried to open it.

'My father's coming up to town on Thursday. I've explained what you want. He'd like to meet you. Lunch, 12.30 on Thursday? The Shangri-La? DS.'

Rebecca sat down and typed her answer. 'Yes. 12.30, on Thursday, at the Shangri-La. Thanks! — Rebecca Lomax.' After she'd sent it off, she wondered if her answer was too short and snappy.

★ ★ ★

Rebecca reasoned that if she was meeting Daniel Seymour's father for lunch in the Shangri-La it was motive enough to wear something nice. She dressed in a pale yellow short jacket with a matching flared skirt, and a slinky tawny top. Elegant high heels and a brown handbag completed the picture. She checked her appearance in the bathroom's full-length mirror that morning and was satisfied. Shortly before lunch she renewed her makeup and set off. She didn't own a car, so she took the underground and walked from the station to the restaurant. It had an illustrious reputation for its food. The chief waiter checked his list. 'Follow me, please.' She threaded her way between the tables after him until he halted, and the smile on Rebecca's face wavered when she saw Daniel Seymour. She hadn't reckoned with him and wondered why he made her flounder like he did. She contemplated the older man standing next to him. He had grey hair, was smartly dressed, and had lively blue eyes in a healthy face. The two men didn't resemble each other very much. Daniel was a head and shoulders taller than his father, and he was also thinner and more austere.

She gave Daniel some attention. 'Mr Seymour! I didn't expect to see you . . . ' She tripped over her tongue. 'Not that it isn't a pleasure, of course.' Her added remark sounded silly. She was usually self-confident, but Daniel Seymour disturbed her poise and she didn't understand why.

His father held out his hand and laughed softly. 'How do you do! I'm Colin Seymour, and you're Miss Lomax? You need information about the family?'

Trying to ignore Daniel Seymour's presence, she shook his father's hand. 'Yes, I'm very pleased to meet you.' She settled down when Colin Seymour gestured her to her chair, and the two men reclaimed their own.

The waiter brought the menu and they all studied carefully what was on offer. Daniel asked politely. 'Like me to choose the wine — or would you prefer to pick something yourself, Miss Lomax?'

She waved the offer aside. 'I'm no wine connoisseur, I only know if I like it or not when I taste it.'

'Red or white?'

'White, and dry, please!' Her hesitant smile evoked little response from him so she concentrated on the menu again. He probably thought every woman who came within arm's length was just longing to fall for him. They were welcome to him as far as she was concerned!

His father looked up and said. 'So many people wrongly pretend to be wine experts, or food experts, these days.'

Daniel gave his father a wry look, although Rebecca was then surprised to hear him agree. For some reason she thought he'd turn out to be a wine expert or food connoisseur. 'Wine tasters have often chosen one of the cheapest wines in tests,' he said dryly. 'I'm positive there's just a great deal of snobbery behind it all most of the time.'

He buried himself behind the large menu again and Rebecca did the same.

They all talked generalities after they'd ordered and then his father asked Rebecca about her job and her background. He asked her to explain what she had in mind for the booklet. Rebecca felt Daniel's sharp and assessing eyes but she refused to let him confuse her thoughts. She straightened her back and answered Colin Seymour's gently pertinent questions gladly. She decided he was a nice man and probably not half as complicated as his son.

Rebecca was still in the middle of her strawberry cheesecake, when Daniel Seymour looked at his watch, crumpled his pristine napkin and placed it next to his plate. 'I have to go.'

Rebecca looked as he touched his father briefly on the shoulder. 'Tell Mum I'll be down for a visit soon.'

'Make sure you do, your life and mine won't be worth living if you don't!'

Rebecca looked down at her silver spoon, and smiled secretly. It was good to know someone could pressure Daniel Seymour. After Daniel left, his father talked about the forthcoming gala and the company history.

'I like the idea of this booklet,' he said, with a smile. 'I'm sure no one has ever thought about compiling one before. I've an absolute pile of old photos and letters and so on, at home. There's even some old ledgers, absolutely ancient they are, crammed with the neatest writing I've ever seen. Not like the kind of writing you see nowadays, that's for sure. It's all packed away into crates and boxes. It would be so useful I am sure, for you to have a good rake through them.'

'I wonder what you might turn up? There's way too much to pack and send — and I certainly would hate to lose any of it. What's to be done?' It was a rhetorical question, and Rebecca sat quietly and looked into her wine glass. At last, the older man nodded his head. 'That's what we'll do!'

He smiled at Rebecca. 'Now that I've met you, I think you should come down and take a look. Take your time and have good root about.'

She smiled at him. 'Are you sure I won't be in the way?'

He brushed her misgivings aside with a decisive shake of his head.

'Not at all!' he said, smiling. 'My wife likes visitors. We used to have a lot of guests when I was still active in the company, but things are a lot quieter nowadays. Stay overnight; that will give you plenty of time to go through it all!'

Rebecca felt apprehensive. From her hesitation, he guessed what was going through her mind. 'It will be easier for you and me, and my wife won't mind.'

She threw caution to the wind. 'All right, thank you, that's very kind.'

'My wife can phone and fix a date. Give me your number?'

She rummaged in her bag and handed him her visiting card. 'There you go,' she said, returning his friendly smile. 'Just phone me anytime on this number, and if I don't answer, then just leave a message on my answering machine. The sooner we get the research done, the sooner the booklet can be completed. I am sure we all want to see the work done as soon as possible.'

'Absolutely right, young lady!' Mr Lomax eyes glinted. 'It's very refreshing to see such enthusiasm — that's what the modern game is all about, enthusiasm! Mind you, if it was just enthusiasm I'd still be working, but it's about energy as well. I can't deny that son of mine has more energy than most, but it's good to see. He really throws himself into his work, and he is passionate about building the business. As I am sure you will find out!'

Rebecca was sure she was going to find something out too — time would tell what it was, and if would be good for her, or not . . .

4

Rebecca studied the passing country-side bathed in the late summer sunshine. She liked Daniel Seymour's father, and hoped his mother really didn't mind her overnight visit. On the phone, she sounded like she was a very pleasant person. When she got out at Ledbury station on the outskirts of the town, Rebecca found a disintegrating, notice plastered to a wall with the number of a local taxi service. She phoned them and ten minutes later with her overnight bag and laptop in hand, she got into a car driven by a cheery looking individual with a cloth cap. 'You called for a taxi?'

'Yes, Leavington Hall, please'.

'That's a fair way outside the town, miss. Cost you a bit!'

Bus-services in the country were infrequent; did they go in that direction? She shrugged. 'That's all right. I expected it to be; it's off the beaten track, isn't it?' Don would have to accept it as extra expenses; she was here on business.

'It's an old house, on the outskirts of a small village about ten miles away.'

The driver chatted as he drove through the streets and left the town. They travelled along lanes bordered by high hedges. Now and then she glimpsed the green pastures and wood-lands beyond. Fifteen minutes later the driver said. 'It's not far now.'

They drove through a pair of wrought-ironwork gates down an avenue lined with old beech trees. Rebecca studied the large house as they drew closer. The grey-stoned, gabled property had an old square tower in its centre with an impos-ing double door and a couple of steps leading up to it. There were add-ons to the left and right of the tower with asymmetrical pointed or slanting roofs. The house had a unique appearance.

She thanked the driver, paid him, mounted the steps and rang the bell. A middle aged woman answered the door just as the taxi disappeared from view.

'Good Morning! My name is Rebecca Lomax.'

'Yes, come in, please! I'll tell Mrs Seymour you're here. I'm Mrs Miller, the housekeeper. Follow me please.'

Rebecca left her overnight bag near the entrance door, took a small package out of her shoulder bag, and then tagged along behind the older woman. She looked around as they went. Superb plasterwork ceilings and richly carved oak panelling were featured throughout the house. There were personal family treasures on display on fine furniture.

They walked down a short hallway. Mrs Miller opened a heavy wooden door. 'Wait here please.' Rebecca nodded. The door closed and she went towards a square alcove with windows overlooking the back of the house. Lovingly maintained sculptured trees were underplanted with seasonal bedding. She noticed herbaceous borders, parterres of wild flowers, and there was also a formal hedged garden not far away with a small fountain and lime trees. Wonderful mature trees were dotted on lush lawns.

The room itself was obviously a family sitting room. It had comfortable armchairs and settees. The curtains framing the windows were beige with a frail pattern of pink and green. The fireplace was mounted by a large mirror, and some shiny occasional tables held scatterings of glossy magazines. There was a half-read book lying face-down on a narrow side table. The room had a great view of the garden bathed in sunshine.

The door opened and a middle-aged woman came in, hand outstretched. She was slim and elegant with light brown hair, good skin and Daniel Seymour's eyes. She and Rebecca were roughly the same height. Her voice was bright and friendly. 'Hello, sorry I kept you waiting; I was in the garden. I hope you had a good journey?'

Rebecca smiled and shook her hand. 'Yes thank you. I was just admiring the garden. It's superb; like a small park.'

'It's my abiding passion. Mabel is bringing us some tea, and then we could take walk around, if you like . . . or perhaps you'd rather see the inside of the house first?'

'I'd love a walk in the fresh air after the train and the taxi.'

'Good!' She pointed. 'That chair is very comfortable.'

Rebecca handed her the package. 'Thank you, for inviting me. I hope you like books? This is about a woman who visits Sicily to find her family roots, and the fascinating characters she meets while doing so.'

Mrs Seymour opened the wrapping and studied the front and back covers. 'How kind! It sounds very interesting. Thank you very much!'

Mrs Miller came in with a tray balanced on one arm. She arranged the china on a table close to Mrs Seymour, and left.

'This is a lovely house, Mrs Seymour. It's so unusual. It looks like several eras of history have been whisked up together.'

Mrs Seymour laughed and the grey eyes sparkled. 'That's a very good description. The tower in the middle is medieval; since then the various owners through the centuries have added bits and pieces without rhyme or reason. Daniel says it's a folly, but it caught my imagination from the moment we found it. I wouldn't want to live anywhere else now.'

'It isn't a folly. It's unique and so unusual. The majority of old houses have fixed lines, fixed styles, fixed periods, this is a fascinating mix.'

'I'm glad you like it, and I agree. We've tried not to alter too much since we moved in, and what we did was done with care. It needed modernising for comfort, but I think we achieved that without destroying its fascination.'

Rebecca gratefully took a sip of tea. 'Do you look after the gardens on your own? That must be a formidable task; it seems to be very big.'

Mrs Seymour shook her head. 'I love gardening, but we have a gardener. Sometimes I think we even need a second one. At certain times of the year when the flower beds are being planted or cleared, or when the trees and bushes are being cut back and shaped, our gardener could work twenty-four hours a day. Ben is Mabel's husband, and he does a wonderful job. Busy all the time, all weathers, all seasons.'

Rebecca enjoyed their walk around the garden. Her hostess told her to explore on her own if she could. 'Don't hide in the library all the time you're here; go outside sometimes. I'll show you to your room now; give you a chance to freshen up. My husband will be back for lunch soon; he had to meet someone from the village about something to do with the parish council.'

On the way to her room she pointed out the way to the dining room. Mrs Miller was setting the table when they peeped in. Afterwards they collected her bag and walked up the wide staircase from the hall and went straight down a short corridor to a guest room.

'Here is your room, my dear,' said Mrs Seymour. The room was square with two large windows looking over the gardens. The windows were open, and voile curtains fluttered gently in the breeze. There was a large double bed, with a pink damask covering, and silk cushions.

Rebecca admired the comfortable room. 'Thank you so much,' she said with a smile. 'I'm sure I will be very comfortable. What a lovely room.'

'Thank you — and it's a comfy bed, too.' Mrs Seymour switched the bedside lamp on and off, in the manner of a hostess. 'That works, thank goodness. I hate it when you have to get out of bed to switch the light off, and bedside lamps are the worst for bulbs going.' She smiled at Rebecca. 'Just make yourself comfortable, and do join us for lunch later.'

* ★ *

When Rebecca went downstairs later, Mr Seymour was waiting in the dining room. He handed her a glass of sherry. 'I've already sorted out most of the stuff I have about the family and the company history. Once you've caught your breath, I'll take you to the library, and you can get to work whenever you like.'

Rebecca decided that even though they were probably extremely rich they were still very nice people. They shared a kind of unspoken familiarity with each other that only came with many years of a good marriage. They talked about people he'd met in the village, and asked her about the journey.

It was a light lunch of tomato soup followed by a salmon salad. Becky was eager to see what Mr Seymour had found for her, but she was also enjoying the situation. She looked around. The dining room was luxurious. It had a moulded plaster ceiling, a superb wooden fireplace surround, and a set of very fine dining chairs around a big oval table.

Every room at Leavington Hall was full of history. She was sure the paintings, china, clocks, glass, and numerous unique items were on display purely for pleasure. It was a real family home with a warm, friendly atmosphere.

Luckily there was a long refectory table in the library so there was plenty of room to spread things out. Mr Seymour had already placed the bundles of papers and photos in neat piles.

'I've pulled out what I think might be of interest to you; starting with the company's beginnings. No photos in those days of course, but there are some written reports. The thicker piles are more up to date, and the closer you get to the present, the more photos there are. A lot have a written explanation on the back. If you're interested in something, and there's nothing written,

I'll do my best to fill in the gaps. I'll leave you to browse through it all for a while.'

Rebecca smiled at him. 'Thanks, it looks like a perfect treasure trove.' She turned eagerly to the waiting documents and photos.

He smiled and turned to go, but Mrs Seymour met him at the door. 'Daniel has just phoned. He was up in Birmingham yesterday; he's making a detour.'

'Staying overnight; or just another flying visit?'

'Staying.'

Mr Seymour nodded. Rebecca tried to ignore the conversation, and focused on the papers in her hand. His parents followed each other out chatting, and the door closed with a soft thud. She couldn't imagine how Daniel Seymour would react to find her here, but his mother must have mentioned there was a visitor.

★　★　★

An hour or so later she'd already picked out lots of useful information. It was easy to see that Seymour's had had a colourful and interesting history. There'd often been times of crisis, but the Seymour family seemed to surmount problems and forge ahead stronger than before.

She took a close look at some recent photos. A lot of them were family snapshots. There were some of Daniel with his parents, and many others with another young man.

Mr Seymour came back. 'Well, how's it going?'

Rebecca gave him a welcoming smile. 'It's amazing how much information you have, especially about the grounding years. I didn't expect that.'

'I think that generation was very proud that they 'moved up' from being farm labourers. They kept every snippets of news about themselves and it was reverently passed down from generation to generation.' He looked at the pile of photos she was holding in her hand. 'I wasn't sure if you needed modern photos for the brochure.'

'They're mainly the present-day generation aren't they? This man is on several of the photos. Is he another close member of the family?'

He took out a pair of glasses from his top pocket and peered at it. 'Yes, that's our other son Gary. He and his wife farm near Hereford. They have three children — my grandchildren!'

'Did he never want to go into the business?'

'No never! Luckily Daniel always did. Danny spent several years travelling the world, after he left the army and we wondered if he'd end up somewhere else, but we wanted him to decide without being pressured into it. Fortunately he came back, and the company goes from strength to strength.'

Rebecca shuffled through the photos. She picked up a studio portrait of Daniel's ex-wife. Her features were flawless. Mr Seymour's eyes followed hers. 'Oh, that's June; that's slipped in by mistake. I expect you know about her?'

'Yes, I've heard of her, and I know that she disappeared in a plane crash, but I can't remember any details. I didn't take any notice of the accident at the time. She's very beautiful'

'Yes, she is, or was. I was always sceptical about their marriage because I didn't think they were suited. She was a butterfly in an artificial world, and Daniel was a worker with his feet on the ground. The divorce was a bit messy and then fate made it more complicated because she vanished like she did.' He looked uneasy as he realised he'd been chatting about family concerns.

Rebecca bared her own soul. It was something she didn't do often, but she trusted Daniel's father instinctively. 'My parents are divorced too. My father left my mother to marry someone much younger. I still don't understand why it happened because my mother is a lovely person and she didn't deserve to be treated like that. I never understood how my father could leave without giving Neil and me a second thought either. I felt like yesterday's newspaper thrown casually into the waste bin. He just forgot about our existence.'

'That must have been hard, but I don't suppose it was quite like that. He's bound to have missed you. I think children suffer most when a marriage breaks up. The adults go their separate ways, no matter who's responsible, but children have no choice — they get shoved one way or the other, and develop scars in the process. I'm not sure if I'm glad or sorry that Daniel and June didn't have any children. If there had been children Daniel would have been solely responsible today. He'd have made a good father. He likes children.'

Mr Seymour stared out of the window for a moment and then at Becky. 'If a marriage is on the rocks, it really is better to split up.' He straightened and looked at his watch. 'Why don't you go for a walk before dinner, and get some fresh air. Daniel is due any minute; so you'll see him then.'

Rebecca shuffled the photos into a neat pile; June Moreland's beautiful face was now on top. 'Thanks, I think I will. I've sorted out quite a lot already. I hope you'll allow me to take what I've chosen with me to copy it? I promise to send it back by registered post as soon as possible.'

He threw up his hands in a gesture of protest. 'No need for that. There's a copying machine in that cupboard over there. Just press the green button and you're away.'

She smiled. 'Really? That's wonderful! I'll show you what I've copied before I leave in case there is something you'd rather I didn't use.' He made a vague motion of protest but Rebecca continued. 'No, please — I'd rather do it like that — then I know I can work with everything without a second thought.'

'There's nothing ominous in there, apart perhaps from something like

June's photo. I have the feeling you wouldn't have used that anyway.'

She shook her head. 'I'll show you what I'm taking and send you a rough copy of the booklet when I'm finished, so that you're in on the final decision.'

'Agreed.' One corner of his mouth curled in a friendly smile.

'I'm off now!' he said. 'There's a cricket match on television I want to catch!'

Rebecca knew Daniel could be a ruthless manager; his father seemed to be a different character altogether — but perhaps Colin Seymour was a more conciliatory character nowadays because he was out of the decision making. Running a big business like Seymour's was never an easy task and managers often had to make unpopular decisions. She began to sort through all the documents and papers that she'd chosen to copy.

Some time later the door opened and revealed Daniel Seymour. The colour rose in her face, and she was glad there was distance between them. He looked relaxed and young; it had a lot to do with the clothes he was wearing. A sports-shirt peeped over the collar of a tan sweater, the beige designer chinos were a perfect fit, and his feet in comfortable loafers made no noise as he crossed the room. He covered the distance quickly with his usual commanding air.

His expression was stress-free and almost friendly, until he spotted the photo of his ex-wife. He stopped abruptly to pick it up and his lips formed into a thin hostile line. His eyes were a sheet of grey ice.

'Who gave you this?' His voice was sharp and demanding.

She wasn't surprised that there was no greeting. His ex-wife was clearly still a very sensitive area. Rebecca didn't want to put his father in the firing range, so she manouvered around with an indirect answer.

'It was among one of the bundle of photos. Got in there by mistake, I expect.' She tried a stiff smile; without success.

He fingered it impatiently. 'I forbid you to use my ex-wife's name. She has nothing to do with Seymour's; never did.'

She felt the rising tension and wished they didn't have to clash. Rebecca disliked the roughness in his voice and the manner of his speech.

'I'd no intention of including your ex-wife. That'd be stupid and insensitive of me; and I'm not stupid or insensitive.' She flattened her palms against herself and waited, trying to stay calm.

His face was pale and the skin was drawn taunt across his cheekbones. 'For your own sake I hope that's the truth.'

Still without uttering a single friendly word, he turned on his heel and the door closed with an audible click as he left the room, the picture was in his hand.

Rebecca let out a sigh of relief as the door closed. Either he was still in love with his ex-wife, or he couldn't come to terms with nasty memories. Someone who rarely faced defeat would find it hard to accept he'd chosen the wrong person to marry. She shrugged; if he wanted to believe she was a sensation-seeker nothing she said would make him believe any different.

5

She decided to go for a walk to clear her head. Mrs Seymour had invited her to explore the garden on her own, and she'd finish the rest of the work after dinner. She looked at her watch. It was now too late to think about catching today's last train. Even if she got a taxi to the station on time, when it reached London the train would be very late, and she hated crossing London on her own in the dead of the night.

She changed her medium heels for a pair of comfortable flat shoes and shrugged herself into her short wind-proof jacket. The day was still fine, but when the sun disappeared, it was obvious that autumn weather was nagging round the corner. She walked quickly across the front courtyard and around the side of the sprawling building towards the back of the house.

There was probably a quicker way through the house, but Rebecca didn't want to go searching. She thrust her hands deeper into her pockets and breathed deeply. The air was wonderful and there was an echoless silence, apart from an occasional bird call from somewhere in the undergrowth. She crossed the carefully nurtured lawns and reached the fence that separated it from the surrounding countryside.

She thought about going further, but decided against it. It was just as pleasant to sit half-astride the wooden fence and enjoy the outlook from here. Behind her was a clean smell of freshly cut grass; ahead was the earthy smell of nature as left to its own devices. She glanced upwards between the moving branches of trees that helped mark the boundary fences.

Clouds were gathering and in the distance they were already obscuring the hilltops. Even if she didn't know the area, she could tell there was rain in the offing. A cool breeze blew across her cheeks and she was glad of the protection of her jacket and the warm brown sweater underneath.

Rebecca's thoughts circled around Daniel Seymour; she mused that being rich had lots of shortcomings. You probably never knew who you could trust and who your real friends were.

You never knew if someone loved you for yourself, or for your money and what it represented. Strands of hair blew across her face. She looked across the fields; the daisies and dandelions had closed their heads for the day.

Walking on, lost in her thoughts, Rebecca was not aware that she was no longer alone — she didn't hear Daniel coming behind her on the walk, and was very surprised to hear his voice drift over her shoulder.

'I saw you from the sitting room,' he said stiffly. 'I came out to say I'm sorry about just now. I'm afraid anything to do with my ex-wife still throws me off course sometimes.'

Sitting on the fence, Rebecca found

herself on a level with his face. Nervously she moistened her dry lips and noted his set face, clamped mouth and fixed eyes. He was wearing a dark brown Barbour coat and had his hands in his pockets. His hair was windswept and she was captivated by the colour of his eyes with their light flecks.

A faint smell of his aftershave or soap wafted across to her. She was surprised by his apology; it probably didn't happen very often. For a moment she studied him and allowed herself to admit he was an extremely attractive man. 'You don't have to explain, Mr Seymour. I understand perfectly.'

'If I found someone prodding around in my private life without my permission, I wouldn't like it either. I promise I won't ever print or write anything you haven't approved of. That's why I wouldn't have made a good journalist; I'm not mean enough to intentionally destroy someone's life.'

He tipped his chin in unspoken thanks and deliberated that she was a very attractive woman without being beautiful in the classical sense.

He asked. 'Is that what you wanted to be?' There was something appealing about the faint hint of freckles on her pale skin and her eyes were undoubtedly her most attractive feature. Sometimes they were hazel, other times a kind of jade. When she was angry they were green fire.

She smiled and was glad to see his face relax as he waited for an answer. 'When I was at university? Yes! I saw myself as a female Don Quixote; righting wrongs, protecting the weak, unraveling political plots. I soon discovered commercial gain came first, even in the world of newspapers and journalism. There are some good reporters who help make things better, but they're few and far between.'

Daylight was fading. Some errant leaves floated from nearby trees as the strength of the wind increased. He looked up and held out his hand to her in a gesture of old-fashioned politeness.

'I think we should go back. It's going to pelt down soon. It's almost time for dinner anyway.'

'Yes, it looks pretty threatening, doesn't it?' She took his outstretched hand and jumped down. His hand was cool and smooth, and she'd an urge to leave it there. She shoved it firmly into her pocket instead. 'Do you change for dinner? I brought a dress, just in case.'

He shook his head and looked amused. 'Good heavens, no. You look perfectly ok as you are. By the way I think we should use Christian names, don't you? Rebecca, isn't it? If you continue to call me Mr Seymour, I won't know if you mean me or my father.'

She inclined her head, and turned towards the house, slightly unnerved by their exchange. He fell in at her side; measuring his long strides to fit her steps. Leavington Hall's silhouette was beginning to merge into the nightfall. She broke the silence. 'I'm going to freshen up before dinner.'

They reached a back door and went into a small square hallway and down a short paneled corridor to the main hall. He hung up his coat and she went up the staircase. She felt slightly better because he'd now defused the situation.

Mrs Seymour had made an entrée of tortellini salad on a bed of radicchio, followed by roast chicken basted in cider and filled with a stuffing of apples and onion. Dessert was a mixture of fresh fruits with vanilla ice-cream. It was all delicious. Mr and Mrs Seymour told her about how they found the house several years ago, and how it had changed since they moved in.

Daniel didn't talk very much and Becky tried to avoid looking in his direction, although she wanted to. She was acutely aware of his presence; he impressed in a way that was hard to define. Perhaps it was just the knowledge about who he was; his position? Deep down Becky knew that wasn't why; it had nothing to do with the managing director of Seymour's. He struck a nerve in her that vibrated. She lingered over her glass of dry Chablis longer than necessary.

Despite the jagged edges of his character, there was something about him that fascinated her, although there was no reason to believe he'd notice her. He could choose his female company from the world of the rich and the jet set; she was a nonentity.

Perhaps other women would do anything to be with him, but she needed to like a man to be interested. Did she like him? She got up.

'That was a lovely meal Mrs Seymour. Thank you!'

'My pleasure! Most of the time, I leave all the cooking up to Mabel, but visitors always give me a valid excuse to invade her kitchen to help her.'

Rebecca folded her napkin. 'Now it's back to work for me.'

'Oh! Must you? I hoped we could have coffee in the sitting room before you disappeared again.'

Rebecca smiled. 'That's very kind,

but I came here to work. I'm sure you've lots of family news to catch up on.'

Her eyes swept briefly across the two men. Mr Seymour gave her a smile; Daniel had an unfathomable expression on his face. She closed the door quietly when she left, and went back to the library.

Sometime later, she was almost finished, the door opened. She wasn't surprised to see Daniel standing there with a glass in his hand. The liquid caught the light as swirled around. 'I thought you'd like something to drink.'

His closeness made her catch her breath, and she took a sip to cover her nervousness. 'Thank you; you're a mind-reader. I've copied all I need. There are loads of interesting items. It'll be hard to pick what to use and what not.'

His dark hair gleamed in the light from the overhead lamp. He smiled, and it softened his features.

'I expect you know more about our family history now than I do!' He paused. 'Dad mentioned you came down by train? Would you like a lift back tomorrow? I've promised to stay for lunch, if you don't mind hanging on till then, it'd save you the hassle of the return journey by train.'

He waited for a reply while her mind was in turmoil. She was still trying to figure out why his mere proximity produced a sort of shock inside her all the time. She'd never known anything like it before. Awkwardly she cleared her throat. 'Yes, gladly!'

He looked at the papers in her hand. 'Then I'll say goodnight Rebecca!'

She was almost glad he was leaving; then she'd be able to orientate her thoughts properly. 'Goodnight!' She couldn't manage 'Daniel' but she said it quietly to herself, after the door had closed.

★ ★ ★

It rained heavily in the night and though she registered the sound, she turned over in the warmth of the soft bed and went back to sleep. She woke later than usual next morning. Although she hurried to shower and dress, it was almost nine o'clock by the time she skipped down the imposing staircase and hurried towards the dining room.

She hoped someone would still be at breakfast and found Daniel studying a Sunday newspaper and drinking coffee. She slipped in and closed the door. 'I'm late. I slept longer than I intended.'

He looked up, folded the newspaper with a rustling sound and laid it to one side. 'Breakfast is any time between 8 and 10!' He gave her the hint of a smile and Rebecca's pulse accelerated considerably.

'You just have to bear in mind lunch is at 12.30 no matter when you had breakfast, or how much you ate! Coffee is in the vacuum jug, or would you prefer tea? I was just about to ask Mabel for some toast. Would you like some, or perhaps you'd like a cooked breakfast? There are cereals, and fresh fruit, yogurt etc. on the sideboard. You can help yourself to any of that.'

She felt a little uneasy to be alone with him so early in the day, but didn't show it. 'No cooked breakfast thanks, but I'd love some toast and honey, and coffee will be great.'

He nodded and disappeared through the doorway, giving Rebecca a couple of moments to adjust to the situation. He was wearing cotton gabardine jeans and a casual sweater over a sports shirt.

It was obvious to her, even though she paid little heed to the snobbery of brand names, that none of his clothes came from a provincial source. She decided that everything about Daniel Seymour was exclusive and special.

She got herself a glass of orange juice, and a bowl of cornflakes, sprinkling the cereal liberally with sugar. There was a pile of newspapers on the sideboard and she took one. It was a bad habit to read at the breakfast table, but when you lived alone, it was a hard pattern to break.

A couple of minutes later Daniel returned with a plate piled high with golden toast. She started to fold her paper, but he lifted his hand.

'Please, carry on — it gives me a legitimate excuse to go on reading mine!'

Rebecca did, and they sat opposite each busy with their breakfast, their newspapers and their thoughts. She felt obliged to say something. 'Your parents have already had their breakfast?'

She took a careful sip of fragrant black coffee from a gold encrusted cup. The hot liquid was rough on the tongue and tasted very good. He looked up and held her glance. 'Yes, I just caught them before they left. They've gone to call on someone they know in the village, before going to church.'

He returned to reading his paper.

Rebecca was just beginning to wonder how to fill in the time between breakfast and lunch when he surprised her with an offer.

'Would you like to go for a walk afterwards? We can do a loop and come back via Burton Wood.'

She was taken aback but answered spontaneously. 'Yes, I'd like that. Even if there are London parks and gardens it's never the same as being in the country.'

'Where do you come from?'

'A small country town, near the Scottish border.'

He looked out towards the garden. 'It's good weather today; an opportunity not to be missed.'

She said hesitantly. 'I hope you don't think you've to entertain me — I can occupy myself if you'd rather be on your own, honestly.'

A flash of humour crossed his face and his head tilted to the side. 'I never go out of my way to entertain anyone! Do you want to come, or not?'

Rebecca mused that mentally she had to stop treating him any differently. He may be managing director of a big concern, but he was only inviting her to go for a walk. If he wanted to avoid her, he wouldn't have offered. He surely knew how to elude company without seeming rude.

She looked at him directly. 'Yes, I do,' she said firmly.

He folded his newspaper and put it aside. 'I have to check if anything special has happened since yesterday, but it won't take long. Back in 10 minutes. OK?'

'No peace for the wicked?'

'It's the price for being boss. It's no big deal; you get used to everything.'

'I'll have another cup of coffee; and then I'll meet you in the hall.'

★ ★ ★

There was the clean fresh smell in the air after the rain of the previous night. There were ruts in the gravel and puddles of rain in the ground as they left the house and turned down a nearby lane.

The wind was fresh but they were

both warmly dressed and it was pleasant to leave the lane and stroll down a well-worn path lined by fringes of trees and straggly bushes. The tall grass along the edges of the way was still soaked by the morning dew.

Now and then Rebecca had to make a detour around shallow puddles; Daniel only had to lengthen his stride.

She was glad to find he responded in a very relaxed way to her comments and questions. They also shared companionable silences that were only interrupted now and then by a bird in the undergrowth, or the faint sounds of a herd of cows in nearby fields. Rebecca avoided topics that would intrude on his privacy, but asked questions about the area and about his parents. In return he asked her politely about her family and her home. They walked for a while, heading as he explained, towards the nearby river.

They came upon the river suddenly; the tumbling water was edged with poplars and was flowing fast after the additional rain from last night. Rebecca pushed some stray strands of auburn hair out of her face and thrust her hands into her pockets as they stopped to view the waters bubbling and racing.

She was acutely aware of him; the way he stood told you he was someone who'd made it in life and he'd also acquired a polished veneer. Their eyes met suddenly and his mouth curved into a slow smile.

He mused that her hair looked like a wreath of rich autumn colours in today's weak sunshine. He turned his eyes toward the river again, and then studied his watch; the metal casing glistened in the sunlight.

'We've plenty of time to go back via the wood! There's no pub around here, otherwise I'd invite you for a drink.'

To her surprise her voice was quite steady. 'If there was, I think the drink would be on me!'

His mouth quirked. 'Perhaps I'll take you up on that another day.'

He was merely being polite of course.

He stared at the flowing water for a few seconds and she wondered what he was thinking about.

They turned and followed the bank of the river for a while before they continued inwards along a footpath that meandered along the side of some fields and ended in a nearby wood. There were some horses in one of the fields, poking around under the branches of an old oak; they eyed Rebecca and her tall companion with interest.

A group of merry hikers shattered the silence for a few seconds as they passed them going in the direction of the river.

The path narrowed and continued onward, snaking its way through the greenery beneath the trees. Pools of shade scrambled over the ground as Rebecca dogged his footsteps.

He looked back sometimes, but neither of them spoke. When they reached home again she was sorry. His company and the walk were worth remembering.

6

Lunch was a relaxed affair. Daniel knew the people his parents talked about and Rebecca didn't feel she was shut out of the conversation. She was a weekend visitor, and it was unlikely they'd meet again. It was decidedly more sensible for Daniel and his parents to have a normal conversation, than to bend over backwards to find insignificant subjects to talk about just for her sake.

They set off after coffee. Rebecca with a thick folder of copied articles and other information, and Daniel with some plastic containers filled with food that would probably block his fridge for days. Rebecca gathered that he had a house in south London, and that it was run by a housekeeper who catered to his everyday needs.

Rebecca doubted if the housekeeper would welcome the food in the plastic containers, but from the way Daniel's eyebrows raised when Mrs Seymour loaded him with the boxes, Rebecca decided it was a well-rehearsed situation and he knew he was facing a losing battle.

His car was luxurious. The smell of real leather seats as she sunk back into their softness, and all the expensive extras, gave her a feeling she was sharing in a lavish lifestyle for a while. He was a good driver; competent and alert. She avoided making conversation, as she felt he was someone who didn't like small-talk. That suited her; she didn't fancy searching for polite topics of interest either. The radio supplied them with entertaining music, and sometimes the passing countryside caught her eye. She spent most of the time reading through her papers.

It surprised her how quickly time passed. Soon they were on the outskirts of London and he asked where she lived. In no time at all he drove into a gap between other cars quite near to her flat entrance. She tidied her folder and pushed it into her briefcase.

Gathering her other belongings she said. 'Thanks for the lift. Right to the doorstep too!' Rebecca added out of courtesy. 'Would you like a cup of tea or coffee, before you make for home?' It cost an effort to hide her surprise when he caught her eye and said.

'Yes, thank you. I would.'

It was the last thing she expected. Her first thought was to remember whether or not she'd left the flat in a decent state. She got out and led the way. Her shoes sounded hollow as she clattered down the steps. Following close on her heels, his footsteps were almost soundless. She searched and found her keys and wondered why he'd accepted.

He had to duck his head and entered into the square-shaped living room. To the right was a small storage room, another led to her bedroom. On the left were doors to the compact kitchen, and to the bathroom. There was a door at the opposite end of the living room leading out to her below-level patio garden. She'd kept the colour schemes bright to compensate for the lack of natural lighting. The walls were lined with pine bookshelves filled with countless books, the settee and easy chairs were cream, their corners filled with multihued cushions. A dining table with a bright table-runner and filigree iron candlesticks, stood on a rush carpet near the patio window; its matching chairs were tucked neatly out of sight beneath it.

Some afternoon sunshine spilled through the rear windows. Rebecca felt slightly flustered, dropped her things on a small side table and went to open the terrace door.

A faint smell of geraniums and myrtle invaded the rooms in a pleasant way. She gestured toward the settee. 'Make yourself comfortable, I won't be a minute. Coffee or tea?'

'Tea, please.'

She nodded and left. Hurrying to

organise everything, as she opened and shut cupboards she wondered if he was just curious about 'how the other half lived'. She shrugged her shoulders, and added a decorative dish with some ginger biscuits. Carrying the tray into the living room, she found him studying her books. He turned.

'You've a very varied taste in books; there's a bit of everything here.'

'Yes, I like anything that's well written. I've always loved books, but we couldn't afford to buy them so I was a sort of permanent fixture in our local library. I love owning books now. Silly isn't it? I ought to sort them out and give the ones I'll never read again to charity shops.'

There was no comment. Rebecca arranged the cups and saucers on the coffee table and he sat down. His long legs stuck out at an angle and he leaned forward to accept a cup of tea. She asked. 'Do you like reading?'

He took a sip, added a spoonful of sugar from the sugar bowl, took another sip, and looked across at her. His eyes were sharp and assessing. 'Yes when I have time.'

'What sort of things?' Her question was artless. She studied his face and focused on the tiny featherlike lines at the corner of his eyes.

He gave her an indulgent look and his eyebrows rose fractionally. 'Oh . . . biographies, autobiographies, history, travel and the occasional thriller.'

Every fibre in her body warned her not to develop too much interest and she was fighting a battle of personal restraint. He was undoubtedly an attractive man, but it was stupid to daydream about someone who led such a different life. Her heart still hammered foolishly when she continued. 'Do . . . do you have any time for hobbies?'

'You mean other than reading?' His light grey eyes held her glance. 'I play golf now and then and usually go for a skiing holiday in winter. I travel a lot because of business, and I sometimes add on an extra day or so if I can and it's somewhere interesting. I enjoy working, so I don't consider life to be split up into a time for work or a time for play.'

Rebecca replaced her cup in the saucer with a clatter.

He changed topics. 'You'll be in touch when you've got a rough draft ready?'

Rebecca noted they were back on neutral ground again. 'Yes, of course. I'll send you my suggestions. Don will want your approval all the way.'

'Your boss has suggested things for the gala dinner. He has good ideas. Unusual ones; without them being foolish or harebrained.'

Rebecca smiled. 'Don is good at his job and he's a first-rate boss too. He always gives us lee-room to think things out. He has an instinct about what'll work, or not. He senses what's right for customers. I don't spin out ideas . . . I come in to it when they're ready to wrap them up in the right kind of wording.'

She didn't realise it, but he liked the

way she supported her boss. Daniel nodded and looked at his watch. He took another sip and put his cup and saucer back on the table.

'Thanks for the tea.' He stood up. 'I'll be hearing from you then?'

She got up too, and looked up into his face. She answered firmly with quiet assurance. 'Yes, of course.'

Somewhere deep inside an irrational voice whispered that she wished he was staying longer.

He strode towards the door, his footsteps silenced by the carpeting. He was so tall he nearly touched the low ceiling, and his presence seemed to overwhelm the small room. At the door he looked back; his expression was inscrutable. 'Enjoy the rest of the day!'

'You too! Thanks again for the lift.'

The door closed with an audible click, and Rebecca was left to unravel her confused thoughts about him. She didn't succeed, and buried herself once more in reading the Seymour family history.

The next time she saw him was when

she went to his offices to hand over some differing versions for the proposed booklet, so that he could decide what he wanted. She could have left the folder at the reception desk downstairs, but emotion launched her into the lift.

She told herself she was only making sure the work landed on his desk and that it had nothing at all to do with seeing him in person. Reaching his office, she handed the folder to his secretary with a brief explanation of what it contained. A sneaky look around and the open door to his office told her she wouldn't get a glimpse of Daniel Seymour today. She pretended she didn't really care.

On her way out she felt a warm glow when she saw him coming down the corridor towards his office with a bundle of papers. When he saw her, his pace slackened for a moment then he came towards her leaving her no room to breathe. Rebecca was motionless; experiencing a gamut of confusing emotions.

His eyes studied her carefully. 'Rebecca, what brings you here?'

She touched one of the buttons on her suit nervously and explained.

He said smoothly. 'I'll try to look through them as soon as I can, although I can't say when. At the moment I'm bunged up with various other things.' He paused. 'I expect you want a definite decision as soon as possible? How about meeting up for a drink after work one evening this week? We can talk about them then.'

She didn't hesitate. 'Yes, if you have time.' Her heart beat accelerated and she was aware that she was holding her breath.

'When do you suggest?' His tone was businesslike, and she answered quickly. 'Tomorrow, or Thursday?'

'Thursday suits me fine. How about The Cockatoo? Know where it is?'

Rebecca moistened her lips and nodded softly. 'Yes . . . roughly. I've heard of it.' His invitation was more than she'd bargained for. She knew she shouldn't be feeding the fire; seeking his company and speculating about him. If she thought about him too much it could lead her down a one way street. Rebecca couldn't understand her growing obsession about him, but she neatly attributed it to the aura usually surrounding a man in Daniel's position.

'I'll pick you up; it's easier that way for us both. About seven?'

★   ★   ★

He opened the car door. She smiled easily and got in to the semi-darkness gracefully; tucking her short skirt into place. Rebecca didn't know how he felt, but was nervous.

Every time she saw him, another bit of her normal composure disintegrated. It was an irrational phenomenon; one that she hadn't experienced before. He was busy concentrating on the evening traffic and Rebecca didn't try to start a conversation, but she did steal looks at

100

him as they progressed. It was only a matter of minutes till they arrived at their destination, and he was lucky enough to find a gap between other parked cars in a nearby side-street. He laid a hand on her elbow as he guided her along the pavement in the right direction and then went ahead of her down some narrow steps lit from above by red and green neon-lighting into the fashionable bar.

Elaborate plant containers flanked the doorway. The lighting was subdued, the music subtle, and the waiters were discreet and soundless. They handed their coats to an attendant, who whisked them away, and then followed a waiter and crossed the carpeted floor to a corner table. They were hidden from curious eyes by the shadows, and they settled on the half-moon leather surface of the bank circling the table. The man hovered with biro and pad at the ready.

'What would you like? How about champagne?'

Rebecca hadn't been offered champagne frequently; in fact never before. She smiled and nodded.

The waiter stated which champagnes were available, and Daniel chose. The man hurried away and returned with a perfectly chilled bottle with a narrow serviette wrapped artistically around its neck and resting in a bucket of ice. As soon as he had filled two flutes he departed.

Daniel raised his glass. 'Here's to us.'

She repeated, 'To us!' The champagne was delicious; she eyed the sparkling bubbles of blonde liquid in the slender glass and took another satisfying sip. Perhaps champagne was over-rated, but there was something special about it. It had never tasted better. She was unaware that Daniel was studying her, and musing that she was uncomplicated, well-informed and easy to be with. In her working capacity she was professional and talented. The two things made her an interesting and noteworthy companion.

She looked around and felt comfortable. Indicating with her head towards a middle-age piano-player who was playing background music on an upright piano, near the bar, she commented. 'You don't hear much live music being played like that these days.'

He smiled a slow smile. 'That's true. It's one of the things that brought me here in the first place — that, and the quiet atmosphere. He's an excellent jazz pianist, but he usually plays popular music — to cater to all kinds of tastes. Let's get the business side of things out of the way; then we can just relax.' He took some loose pages out of his breast pocket. 'I like your style. I've marked the paragraphs I fancy. If you combine them, and let me see it again, I'll give you my final blessing.'

Rebecca took the sheets from his outstretched hand, avoiding direct contact. She glanced at them briefly; at the passages marked with brackets boldly in dark blue ink. 'Yes, of course. I'll send it back as soon as possible.' She tried to push the papers into her handbag, but needed to fold them again to do so.

He watched her silently and conversation came to a temporary halt for a second. She was surprised when he asked. 'I hope you don't have to face a furious boyfriend because of our meeting?'

Rebecca shook her head; her hair moved back and fore slightly. The colour in her face rose a little. 'He wouldn't be a decent boyfriend if he didn't trust me, would he? But there's no one at present. I've just separated from someone.'

He picked up the flute with his slender fingers and took a measured sip of champagne. 'How long were you together?'

'Oh . . . roughly six months.'

'So it was quite serious?' Daniel was surprised by his interest and by the brief feeling of envy.

Rebecca shrugged. 'On the face of it perhaps, but no — I discovered it wasn't at all serious — otherwise I'd be sorry that it ended, but I'm not.'

He changed the topic of conversation. 'Would you like something to eat? They do some very good snacks. Not cordon bleu meals — but very tempting appetisers. Very tasty!'

'No thanks.'

He waved a waiter away and extracted the bottle from the bucket of ice cubes himself. 'Then have some more champagne. I'll pass because of driving.'

She wrinkled her nose. 'I can't resist another glass, but I hope you don't think I'll finish the bottle on my own.'

The dark brows arched mischievously. 'Perhaps they have a 'doggie-bag' for bottles? That would be a good idea!'

They both smiled, and began to talk easily about the latest headline in the evening paper and one theme led to the next. They both relaxed. Daniel cleared his throat. 'Actually I was wondering what you were doing next weekend?'

Her green eyes widened and her lips

parted in surprise. 'Why?'

'I'm . . . I have to personally take a look at a new processing system at one of our production centres. A lot of research and work has gone into a new product, and they're doing the first trial run next Saturday. I wondered if you'd like to come with me?'

His offer worried Rebecca; she looked down for a second, hesitated, then looked up again and said shaking her head, 'I really don't think it's a good idea.'

He gazed at her with a bland smile. 'Why not?'

'I'm flattered, and I'm sure you've successfully asked millions of delighted girls to spend a weekend with you before, but a cosy twosome like that is not my scene.'

His jaw clenched. 'Actually I've not asked many women to spend any time with me since my divorce, and no-one has had an offer to spend a weekend with me. My mind boggles at the prospect of a million women.'

A tremor on her lips, she coloured. 'I'm sorry. I didn't intend to sound offensive in any way. It was perhaps presumptuous of me to just assume that you meant . . . ' Her voice trailed off and her colour increased as he held her glance. She swallowed a lump in her throat. ' . . . In a roundabout way you're my employer and we ought to keep everything straightforward and above board.'

He looked almost amused. 'I don't know exactly what you presumed I meant, but I merely thought you would like to see where Seymour started from. The small factory in question is in a lovely area of the countryside, and a visit to the hotel would give you extra insight into the company's beginnings. It was Seymour's first dispatching house in former times and as you mention it in your brochure I thought you might be interested to see what it looks like today, in real life. It also happens to be quite near to my brother's farm.'

With tongue in cheek as he observed her growing embarrassment, he continued. 'I intended to book separate rooms, tie up the business, and visit my brother. I was going to leave it up to you if you'd like to meet him and his family or not. To be perfectly honest I also thought it was a good opportunity for us to get to know each other a little better, but with quite innocent intentions. Just a pleasant weekend break, with no strings attached.'

Rebecca laughed shakily and turned bright pink. 'When you put it like that I'm sorry I was so guarded.' To be honest, she was thrilled by the prospect of spending time with him. She met his eyes and managed a reply. 'Then I'd like to come. A weekend in the country would be lovely.'

Daniel was intrigued. He usually found women fell over themselves to cultivate his company. He knew it was often because of what his name stood for, or what his money could buy. He hoped to heaven that it also sometimes had to do with him as a person too. He had no illusions; he realised his position and affluence attracted a certain kind of female; the kind with purely ulterior motives and who were willing to pay for his company with their bodies.

It was intriguing that Rebecca Lomax was more frightened by his background and the power it gave him than finding it an added attraction. His spontaneous idea to ask her along seemed a more interesting prospect now than before.

That week Rebecca was a bundle of nervous expectation. On the one hand she wanted to spend time with him, and on the other she wondered if it was sensible. He clearly didn't dislike her, otherwise he'd never have considered taking her along, but he was a man who always planned ahead. She wondered if she was part of a chess game where her opponent had already worked out the next three moves, and she was about to make her first. Perhaps his intentions were innocent, and harmless, but then again . . . She couldn't help speculating.

They'd agreed to travel down on Friday evening after work. With a feeling of butterflies in her stomach, they passed the journey in easy familiarity; each talking about various minor happenings since they last met. Daylight was fading fast, and it was fairly late when they reached the sprawling Cotswold village. The hotel reminded Rebecca of a large manor house and once inside she noticed it had retained a lot of the trappings of a late medieval prosperity; gabled roof, elaborate mullioned windows, and centered arches over the doorways.

Inside, the rooms were in rhythm with the age of the building, but the rooms had been discreetly modernised to keep in step with visitors' expectations. A hushed and comfortable atmosphere reigned. This was partly due to the very attentive staff, and partly because the hotel automatically had a special ambiance that was rooted in sheer age. Rebecca acknowledged that being in the company of the owner didn't lessen the attention she got either.

She loved the obvious luxury of her room with its en-suite bathroom, and she spent the short interval they'd agreed on to freshen up.

Rebecca left her overnight suitcase untouched and re-joined Daniel in the small restaurant downstairs.

He was studying the menu, but he got up, when she came towards him and held her chair politely until she was seated. His appearance and the fact that he was her partner this evening made her tremble inside, but outwardly she hoped she looked as calm as ever.

He'd changed his business suit for less formal clothes and he sat down opposite and unfolded his starched white serviette with a flourish.

She looked around the flagged room with its large open fireplace. The flickering flames from the logs that smelled of fragrant apples danced wildly around the surrounding stone-work.

Rebecca sighed contentedly. 'This is really lovely!'

'I agree with that. Even although I know Seymour owns it, I still think it's quite special. I'm glad that it still pays its way; if it didn't I'd have a hard job to defend it. Hotels everywhere have a difficult time to break even these days.'

'Was it originally a manor house? That's what it reminds me of.'

'I think it was once a merchant's town house. The wealth of the Cotswold came from sheep, and many large houses like this one were built at the peak of prosperity. Later, when Seymour founded their transport business, this building was already very old. They rented it cheaply from the owners, because it was empty and no one else wanted it at the time. The position was ideal for the family's needs because it happened to be next to one of the main local highways then, and it also had a large stabling area out the back.'

'Most of the stables have now been pulled down to make room for other things. As soon as the family made money they bought the house, and later bought the farm not far away, where my great, great grandfather formerly worked as a labourer.' His face took on a dry expression.

'I suspect that was a move made more for reasons of personal satisfaction, than for sensible commercial motives. My brother took over the farm over ten years ago when the previous farmer who worked it for us went into retirement, and he's added more acreage year by year since then. He breeds livestock and grows barley.'

The waitress came with the menus and for a while they concentrated on ordering their meal. When that was out of the way, Rebecca asked. 'So actually things have gone full circle. Your brother is the farmer at the farm where it all started. Is it still company-owned?'

Daniel laughed softly. Despite the fact that it made her pulse quicken,

Becky wished he'd do it more often.

'No. Gary is his own boss. I don't think he'd have taken it on, unless the farm was his own, lock stock and barrel! He's only interested in the Seymour-Companies in an abstract way. He has to pay some attention to what is going on, because he gets dividends like the rest of the family and he is part of the board, but apart from attending meetings he doesn't want to get involved, and isn't really interested. He'd never feel happy working in business; he's not an office type of person at all. I suspect that he thinks one of his children may develop an interest in the company and want to join it one day, and that's why he's trying to keep up a semblance of involvement. I'd welcome any of them, but it's still early days because they are still all youngsters.'

'Would you like to meet him and his family? I told him I was bringing someone down with me this weekend, so they wouldn't be surprised if you turned up with me.' He hastened to add. 'You don't have to; it's up to you entirely.'

Rebecca was already far too fascinated about the man and his background to resist the temptation. 'Yes, if you're sure I'm not in the way!'

Daniel relaxed and nodded. 'Good! I have to go to the factory tomorrow morning, but I should be back by lunchtime. Perhaps you'd like to explore the village, or just relax at the hotel? They have a very attractive garden out back with some sheltered corners. With a warm rug it's a perfect place to relax and enjoy the country, I can recommend it. We'll drive out to the farm after lunch.'

The waitress brought the first course. They were both hungry and appreciated the excellent cooking. After the meal they went into the lounge bar and shared a drink. Soft music played in the background and a soft murmur from other guests provided a comfortable background. They had no difficulty in finding topics to talk about. They had parallel attitudes on various subjects and differed on others, but either way it made no difference. Rebecca had seldom felt so at home with a man before. It wasn't just because Daniel was good looking; he was sophisticated, self-assured and an intelligent man who expressed himself well, but also knew how to listen to and accept other people's opinions. She liked him, and liking was turning into something more.

He made no move to touch her or delay their parting at the narrow bend of the upstairs corridor. Becky thought she'd be mulling the evening in her mind for long time, but she didn't. She fell asleep instantly and slept like a log.

7

The surrounding countryside was beautiful, although she realised the peaceful picture of rural bliss was misguiding. Without any personal experience of farming she still realised there must be an awful lot of work involved in running a farm like this.

Daniel had immediately been conscripted into playing a game of football with his oldest nephew. Daniel's normally neat and tidy hair was flopping back and fore onto his forehead as he ran about. Without his inhibiting sports jacket, he tried to keep pace with a twelve year old boy who wasn't just a fanatical football fan but also a fully-fledged member of his school's junior football team. Daniel looked in her direction; half-bent over and breathing deeply; with his hands resting on his hips.

He grinned at her and shrugged, before he once more centered his attention on his nephew, with a determined expression. She was sure he somehow intended to get the ball past his nephew and between the goal-post (two conveniently placed rubbish bins).

Rebecca's pulse automatically spiralled when she noticed how relaxed he was, and how happy he seemed to be. He was evidently having fun. No one in the board room could ever imagine the hard-bargaining manager they knew could loosen up like this and become a big-kid himself for a while.

She would like to have gone on watching, but Gary invited her inside, and it would have been impolite to refuse. He offered to show Rebecca around while his wife finished off preparing them a meal.

After an interesting tour of a building that was full of history but which had still managed to remain a family home, Gary stood next to her on the long red-bricked sprawling terrace, looking beyond the tamed garden to the fields surrounding the house.

Beef cattle were grazing in contented groups, looking from where she stood very much like toy animals. Gary was clearly very curious about the woman his brother had brought along on one of his seldom visits.

He was as tall as Daniel but broader with muscles hardened by lots of physical work. His ash-blond hair was short and wild and he had lively blue eyes. 'Daniel went to the factory this morning, didn't he? Did you go with him?'

She shook her head vigorously. 'No. I explored the village and was pleasantly surprised. I thought it was so small, that I'd find next to nothing. I didn't expect to find so many specialist shops.'

Gary pushed his hands in his pocket and grinned. 'Yes, they're mostly owned by families who've run them for several generations. Traditionalists who believe in quality and brand names — well, that's what my wife tells me. I try to

119

avoid shops as much as I can. She picks things and brings them to me to choose! That's something Daniel and I have in common — we both dislike shopping — but he can't avoid it like I can. In his position, he has to keep up appearances and look the part.'

'I wouldn't know; although somehow I can't imagine him frittering away much time in a shop!'

He laughed. 'No, neither can I.' There was a short pause. 'How long have you known each other?'

She gave him a candid look. 'Not long and not very well. I work for a public relations company that's handling the company's 150th Celebrations and he thought I'd like to see where the Seymour Company started from.'

'Oh . . . I see! I thought you and he were . . . Nevertheless, I'm sure he must like you — Daniel's never made a habit of bringing someone when he visits us. In fact I can't remember many apart from June. She came several times, but that was years ago now. You know about her, about June . . . ?'

Rebecca nodded. 'Not very much. He never mentions her, and I know it's a sore point with him, so I steer clear. I'd have to know him a lot better to talk about her to him and it's really none of my business.' Rebecca crossed her arms over her chest.

Gary stared ahead and looked across the distant fields. 'I can understand why she attracted him, she was an extremely beautiful woman, and she was intelligent too, but very calculating, and with a very explosive personality. She did make an effort to fit into the family in the beginning, but it didn't last long.'

'Once they were married it was soon clear that our kind of quiet lifestyle bored her, and she was often irritable if she had to spend time with any of us. She made no bones about the fact that she loved the bright lights and parties more than any of our family get-togethers.' He shrugged.

'I think Daniel had difficulties accepting that from the start because my mother has always made a great effort to keep family ties as tight as possible. Even through all the years when the business took up most of my father's time, she always managed to keep us together on birthdays, Christmas etc etc.'

'After Daniel married it wasn't long before he was forced to choose between the family and accompanying June, because she always seemed to have other plans. I think that was when the first thread of their marriage began to unravel.'

'She didn't understand how she was creating conflicting loyalties in him. He'd grown up as part of a close family, whereas June avoided her family like the plague. We met them at the wedding, and they seemed to be very nice people, but clearly June had problems with them.'

'Later when things got worse and she and Daniel had begun to drift apart, the gutter press had a great time reporting her escapades at wild parties, especially if Daniel wasn't present.'

'From then on there were always rumours that she was having an affair. Daniel couldn't ignore it, especially when he found out that some of the reports were true. Then their marriage broke down completely and it ended with an unpleasant mud-slinging match in court.'

Rebecca felt very uncomfortable talking about Daniel, but her curiosity got the better of her. 'Hmm! That must have been very tough for him. He's not someone who'd accept personal defeat easily is he?'

'He retained his cool for the sake of the company, even though I'm sure he often longed to hit back when the press started printing all kinds of gossip about him as well as June,' Gary went on.

'He did try to save something out of the remains when things began to disintegrate, and I know that right up to the end he was prepared to make another real effort if June promised to do the same, but things had gone too far by then.'

'I can't remember what was in the newspapers at the time.,' said Rebecca. 'It's a long time ago and I wasn't interested. I certainly never expected to meet Daniel Seymour in person, or perhaps I might have paid more attention.'

'Ah well! They divorced, and as fate would have it, she disappeared soon after but it hardened Daniel,' Gary said, and shook his head sadly. 'He's not likely to trust another woman so easily again.'

Something moved in the half-darkness of the living room behind them. Daniel came out. His lips were firmly unsmiling, and his expression was blank. Rebecca guessed he'd been an unwilling listener to the end of their conversation, and she felt terribly guilty.

His voice was cold and crisp. 'Tea is ready! Sue sent me to fetch you!'

Gary and Rebecca turned and followed his stiff figure back inside and through the rambling rooms to where Gary's wife had a meal waiting for them. Gary and Rebecca looked furtively at each other and felt embarrassed.

The three children covered any awkwardness. The youngest was at an age when fooling about was an interesting pastime, the middle one failed to recognise that his younger sister was pulling his leg, and the older son, still fresh from the improvised football game with his uncle, was just itching to get away from the constraints of the tea-table and the silly behaviour of his younger brother and sister to return to the far more important task of training his dog for the local agricultural show.

Despite the fact that Daniel may have been annoyed with her and his brother, Rebecca noted he'd put it aside to enjoy the noise and the unbridled energy of his nephews and niece.

His expression was very indulgent and he tried to cushion the effect of his sister-in-law's attempts at keeping discipline at the table. Rebecca decided he'd make a good father; he'd be lenient and patient. She decided it would be a great pity if he never had any children of his own.

It was a typical farm-house tea; too much of everything, a lot of it was home produce, and all of it was delicious. The four adults remained a long time comfortably chatting about the farm and the locality long after the youngsters had been given permission to leave. Rebecca liked Gary's wife, Sue.

She was pretty with dark curls, a fresh complexion, a slim figure, and an engaging manner. It was hard to believe her oldest son was nearly twelve. There was a feeling of harmony and under-standing between Gary and Sue.

Rebecca mused that the Seymour's were typical examples of modern-times. One of the Seymour sons had a happy marriage that was working out well, and the other son's marriage had gone completely haywire.

Dusk was gathering as Daniel and

Rebecca drove back through the high-bordered roads back to the hotel. They weren't hungry and agreed that they didn't want a meal at the hotel's restaurant that evening, so there was no hurry. Rebecca noticed he was rather withdrawn, but she did expect they'd have a drink together before they parted.

Her hopes came to nothing. He parked and locked the car, and strolled with her towards the hotel entrance.

Suddenly he paused, and turned to face her. Rebecca stopped automatically and looked up at him. Some inner voice warned her of what he was about to say. The possibility had existed since he came to fetch Gary and her for tea.

His face was in the shadows, but Becky could imagine his expression when she heard the clip and precise tone of voice.

'I thought you realised that I'd be extremely annoyed if I found you try to dig out personal information about my family, especially about my ex-wife. I heard you talking about her to Gary. It seems you promise one thing and do another.'

Her eyes sparkled with anger. 'I assure you that I did not 'dig' for information about anyone. Yes, I did talk about your wife to your brother, but he brought her name into the conversation not me. I just commented on what he said.'

'Am I supposed to act like a zombie when people talk to me about your wife?' She tossed her head and her hair bounced up and down.

'Let's get something straight once and for all,' she went on. 'I don't care one way or the other about your ex-wife, your divorce, or about what happened before or after.' Her tone grew sharper.

'It's all entirely your business not mine and I've never tried to take advantage of you or anyone else you know! I've told you that before!'

'For what it is worth, I think that you've a chip on your shoulder ten foot high about your ex-wife and your marriage, and that you're hypersensitive about what happened. You invited me to come this weekend, but I certainly didn't expect to be muzzled just to keep your ego intact!'

'There are thousands of other couples who end up in exactly the same boat that you were in, every year. After a while both parties move on and start to live again because there's no alternative than to do that. It seems you are still wallowing in self pity about what happened; probably because you're so used to success you can't accept the fact that something in your life failed — no matter whose fault it was.'

'It's absolutely ridiculous.' He was standing stiffly, his expression half-hidden, his eyes sparkling like pieces of ice in the half-light. Rebecca ploughed on.

'Not many people will even remember your wife's name any more.' Rebecca hoisted her bag onto her shoulder impatiently. She felt better, even though he was now listening to her with a masked expression.

Confronting him with words he wouldn't want to hear was an unthankful task, especially because he was indirectly her present employer. She turned swiftly on her heel and hurried towards the hotel entrance and straight up the stairs.

On the way, grabbing the balustrade, she paused for a fraction of a second, and wondered if she'd gone too far. She decided she hadn't; she'd made up her mind long ago to be truthful as much as was possible. It wasn't always a popular thing to do, but she wasn't interested in being popular, she was interested in honesty. It was easier to be truthful than to act a charade.

Being her employer didn't mean that she couldn't tell him what she thought. He couldn't pretend she wasn't doing her job properly, and that was all that mattered. Rebecca continued, on her way.

Still standing outside, Daniel watched

her departing figure through the glass entrance doors until she disappeared. He walked slowly after her and saw his own outline. He ran his fingers through his hair, and gradually the expression of stiffness and disgruntlement slacked.

Rebecca Lomax interested and also baffled him. He'd never met anyone quite like her before.

She was very attractive and intelligent, and she was someone who didn't believe in half-truths; he liked that. He knew there was a definite underlying flow of electricity between them, but he had no intention of making the same mistake twice. True, she did intrigue him but he didn't need another permanent relationship. He'd believed June was someone who would fill his life forever and he'd made his first big mistake

Rebecca Lomax wasn't going to be big mistake number two. There were enough other women who'd fill the moments when he felt there was something missing in his life.

★ ★ ★

His voice was in neutral shades next morning when she joined him for breakfast. He was spreading butter generously on some toast. The butter melted and ran over his fingers as he ate. He sucked them clean and then wiped them again on the pristine damask serviette. 'Morning Rebecca! How did you sleep?'

All her intentions to remain distant and aloof with him failed, and it also bothered her that he knew perfectly well she'd intended to be annoyed with him. His grey eyes sparkled, so she formed her lips into a stiff smile and kept her face as natural as possible; neither of them referred to yesterday. 'Very well, thanks!'

He nodded and took another generous bite of toast. Absentmindedly he mused as he studied her that the dark green suit she was wearing was very tasteful and it flattered her face and colouring. 'I thought we could visit somewhere on the way back, or do you want to go straight home?'

Surprised by the turn of events she ignored the feeling of slight euphoria that he wasn't angry with her, and answered. 'Where were you thinking of going?'

He lifted his shoulder slightly. 'I haven't decided — I'm open to suggestions.'

'I presume you are talking about stately homes or famous gardens?'

He picked up a thick guide from a nearby chair. 'I borrowed this enormous book from reception. I've stuck bits of paper in places that are directly on route. You choose!'

It turned out to be a lovely day that she looked back on with pleasure. Rebecca relaxed completely. It was easy to enjoy his company among the anonymous company of the other visitors.

He looked pleased with himself and the world in general. They visited a beautiful Tudor manor house and wandered around the gardens afterwards. He showed a surprising amount of knowledge about the Tudor period, and Rebecca's admiration and respect grew. They had lunch in the manor house's small restaurant, and he was amused, and taken slightly aback, when she insisted on footing the bill.

After, the journey was comfortable with no awkward moments. They had more in common than she ever imagined, and topics of conversation included politics, travel, books and music flowed back and fore. They didn't always agree, but that made things all the more interesting and full of spice.

Rebecca was almost sorry to reach home. He could be autocratic, demanding, and overpowering, but also attentive and charming. He was a kaleidoscope of characteristics.

She asked him in for coffee, but he refused. She wasn't surprised, even though she was still disappointment. She took her overnight bag and gave him a quick smile.

'Thanks for a lovely weekend, Daniel,' she said formally. 'It was a beautiful part of the countryside. I'll be in touch as soon as I've finished the booklet.'

His grey eyes were speculative. 'You're welcome. Yes let me know when you have something new. Oh . . . I'm due to go to Sweden on business. If you have a prototype and I'm not there, give it to Irene. I'll get it when I'm back.'

His words disappointed her; she hadn't expected him to be so off-hand. Her heart was heavy and her stomach swirled in confusion. Rebecca resisted the temptation to ask when he was going, and when he'd be back. She didn't wait for him to drive away either.

Hurrying down the steps to let herself into her empty flat she listened as the engine died away into the distance. The weekend she'd spent in his company meant nothing to him after all; she came down to earth with a thud.

Daniel ran his hand over his face, and told himself it was all for the best. Business and pleasure didn't mix.

8

Rebecca concentrated on producing text worth reading. The final version was good, even she knew that. She sent a copy to Daniel's father and he phoned back, full of praise. Daniel also approved; his signature was flourished across the provisionary versions. Becky had seen him during visits to his offices to see various people, and he'd visited their offices once.

They managed a nonchalant nod, but no personal talk. Rebecca tried to put him out of her mind, and some days she almost succeeded.

Everything went well. To Rebecca's surprise, Don, she and Roger received an official invitation to the company's main celebration dinner-dance. Mostly only someone like Don got a look in. The gala evening was held in a large hotel that had a ballroom big enough to accommodate the numbers involved. She, Don, and Roger sat at a table with some strangers, towards the back of the room, but they had a good view of what was happening up front. Rebecca could see Daniel's family and other board members at the same table.

Daniel's speech was concise — about the company's position in today's global world sprinkled with amusing anecdotes about the company's past. He announced finally that the Seymour family was setting up a foundation to improve prospects for young people living in the poorer areas of big cities. His announcement was met by a buzz of approval and loud clapping.

From the comments she heard, she could tell that the Seymour family, and Daniel in particular, was admired and respected. The company was doing well, and he'd already proved his abilities to guide the firm through economic ups and down for some years already.

The three of them had agreed beforehand to leave after the speechmaking. Rebecca was sorry she wouldn't be around when the dancing started — but there was little chance he'd ask her to dance, anyway. He was too busy with his official duties. She saw his tall figure already making the rounds. She told Don she was going to say hello, and goodbye, to Daniel's family and she'd be straight back. He nodded.

'Go ahead! We'll get the coats, and meet you downstairs.'

Rebecca threaded her way to the main table, and was rewarded with a warm welcome. They asked her to join them, but she explained that she was about to leave with her boss. Rebecca ignored the two empty chairs at the table. She hadn't seen Lucinda Martin, but it was logical that Daniel wasn't here alone. She concentrated on the people present.

'We may not meet again so I didn't want to leave without saying goodbye, and thank you all for being helpful, kind and welcoming.'

Mr and Mrs Seymour eyed her sympathetically and smiled generously. Mr Seymour said. 'You and your company did a really good job.' He gestured around with his hand. 'It's all gone off like clockwork.'

Mrs Seymour quickly added. 'It's a small world Rebecca. Who knows, perhaps we'll meet again! I hope so.'

Gary added. 'If you're ever near the farm, you're welcome to call. We'll be glad to see you anytime.' His wife nodded in agreement.

Rebecca asked. 'Did Simon win the dog-training competition? I wondered how he got on.'

Gary answered with a wide smile. 'He got a silver medal! It's made him determined to get gold next year!'

Rebecca smiled back. 'From the impression I got, he's very determined once he's made up his mind, isn't he?'

Tongue in cheek Gary's wife said. 'It's a Seymour trait; they never give up.'

Rebecca laughed softly. 'Good thing too! Hope you enjoy the evening.'

Gary quipped. 'I will as long as Sue doesn't drag me onto the dance floor.'

Becky smiled and lifted her hand in farewell. With a slight sensation of disappointment, she joined Don and Roger. They walked to Don's car and he gave them a lift home.

There was no plausible reason for her to see Daniel again. The last couple of weeks there'd been no chance for private conversation. He was always extremely busy. Rebecca wished that she'd had the chance to say goodbye to him properly at the gala.

She liked him more than she cared to admit. She comforted herself with the idea of sending him a short e-mail, as a concluding gesture.

To her surprise he phoned back. Her pulse increased and colour flooded her cheeks when she heard his voice. They talked a while about the success of the gala evening and she was breathless when she heard. 'I was wondering if you'd like to go to the theatre one evening? There's a new play everyone is talking about. I thought you might like to see it?' There was a pause. 'I didn't get the opportunity to say thank you for your part in the work for the company celebrations. You'd disappeared before I had the chance.'

She felt like a gauche teenager accepting her first ever date. She didn't question his motive, just decided to joyfully agree. 'Thanks I'd like that very much.'

'Good! Is this Saturday ok?'

Rebecca wondered briefly for a moment if she should have hesitated, but she didn't. 'Fine!'

'I'll pick you up at about six.' Daniel mused that he'd have to pay through the nose for two tickets at such short notice, but it would be worth it.

The play was good, but she was so aware of Daniel at her side that she didn't give it the attention it deserved. He invited her back to his house for a drink. Her tilted head and expression made him add. 'I promise I won't ask you to look at my etchings.'

Rebecca laughed and nodded; her eyes sparkled in anticipation.

A short time later they were standing in his living room, Rebecca watched as he took some books out of a tall rosewood cabinet standing on the side of the room and handed them to her. She looked at the title. 'Good heavens! I ought to wear gloves.'

He shrugged. 'All books are made to be handled, even first editions.'

'She turned one book round reverently. This is wonderful. I never thought I'd actually hold them! I read that a first printing of Pride and Prejudice like this was auctioned off for twenty-three thousand pounds not so long ago.'

He enjoyed watching the deference in her face. 'Collecting first editions is an interesting pastime. Nowadays individual collectors have a hard time because they have to compete with big libraries and museums. Supply and demand sets the end price, but the fight to get what you want is the enjoyment.'

She opened a couple of pages of one and studied them carefully. 'Why do you collect? There must be more profitable ways of investing your money.'

He shrugged. 'Perhaps . . . in fact that is probably true, but I enjoy tracking them down, and competing. I always set myself a limit and stick to it. If I keep them in optimal conditions, they won't lose value. They'll gain.'

'And if your home goes up in smoke you lose every penny in seconds.'

He showed no sign of irritation. 'They're insured against theft or fire. I'd feel real regret, but it's a risk you take. The other alternative would be to put them in a fire-proof vault; then no one would ever see them. What's the point of that?'

Rebecca tilted her head to the side to look at the titles of some of the other books in the display cabinet. '*David Copperfield, Treasure Island, A Tale of Two Cities, Wuthering Heights*! Heavens! All first editions?'

'Yes.' He was amused by her amazed expression.

Rebecca gave him the books back. '*Pride and Prejudice* has to be my all-time favourite because it's a classical love story, and because Jane Austen was a wonderful observer of her times.'

Daniel put the books back in the display cabinet. He locked it with a small key attached to his key-ring and routinely checked on the humidity display. Rebecca mused there was a small fortune on those shelves.

He turned and gestured towards a sofa. 'Would you like a drink?'

'Please.' She sat down; tucked her legs neatly to one side. He asked, 'White wine? Dry?' She nodded.

Bottle and glasses were on a black lacquered side-table. Next to them was a crystal vase filled with tall white lilies. He poured pale wine into two long-stemmed glasses, handed her a glass and lifted his own. 'Here's to us!'

'To us!' Rebecca took a sip and

enjoyed the subtle fruity flavour on her tongue.

'I was down in Leavington last weekend, visiting my parents. The trees are bare skeletons and the garden is cleared for the winter.'

Rebecca smiled easily. 'Your mother obviously loves it, and that makes it all worthwhile, I expect. Did they have a garden when they lived in London?'

'No, they had a large penthouse with a big terrace, but I think she always longed for a garden. She comes from a village in the Cotswold and was delighted if they could get out of London and into the countryside for a break. She'd never be able to manage a garden of that size on her own of course, but my father is happy to be able to indulge her now, to make up for when she had to make do with potted plants. It was the reason they bought the house — she fell in love with the gardens.'

She glanced around pointedly. 'You have a lovely house too Daniel. It's beautifully decorated and very soothing on the eye.'

He spread his arms expansively; the wine in his glass sloshed back and forth. 'One of the perks of having money is being able to buy nice things.' He took a seat on an opposite sofa. They were separated by a low glass table. 'But I must admit I feel very comfortable. I bought the house after my divorce. It's a quiet area, my neighbours are nicely communicative and also fairly reserved, and it's far enough from the office to stop me being a workaholic.'

Rebecca laughed softly. 'You seem to be completely proficient and efficient.'

'Really?' He lifted his eyebrows and there was a quirk to his mouth. 'I have to disillusion you, I'm very human. I admit I'm very resourceful in making people believe I'm well-organised and almost faultless, but they'd all be very shocked if they could see how disordered my life is sometimes. You should see my sock drawer!'

'I can't believe it! Most people stand in awe of you.'

'Do they? Do you?'

She felt flustered by the question. 'Admittedly, it was easier for me to handle things when you were just Don's customer. I could shove you into a convenient folder and close it if I felt confused by your attitude or your actions.'

'And now?' He fingered the stem of his glass.

She had to concentrate on her answer. She swallowed hard. 'I don't think I was ever awed, I hope not anyway — not in the sense of being afraid of you. I was in awe of the image of the managing director and I respected what you did and how you did it — but since I got glimpses of the man behind the business mask, I think I like him a lot better.'

He leaned forward, opened the button on the jacket of his midnight blue dinner suit, and loosened his black tie. His eyes had a brilliance that almost made her shiver. 'Perhaps you'd like to know what I like about Rebecca Lomax? Basically it's her honesty. Most people prefer to live with half-truths. Do you realise we're very alike because we say what we think? Anything else is compromise and leads nowhere.' There was a pause. 'Would you like to see the rest of the house?'

'Yes, of course.'

'Then follow me!'

Rebecca did. They did a swift tour of the ground floor, and she was impressed by the luxury. Despite the opulence everywhere there was still a comfortable feeling to the rooms. The only place that seemed rather sterile was the kitchen; it was in shades of black and white, and the sink and electrical items were stainless steel. It needed the softening touch of someone who used it as part of their lifestyle. Some plants, some cookery books, less precise neatness everywhere. She was sure that Daniel seldom used it. He had a housekeeper, and she kept it in a state of efficient perfection. For a moment she thought how she'd bring it to life.

He viewed her as she moved through the rooms. Her comments were sparse, but he sensed that she liked his home. She trailed her hand over the shiny balustrade as they went up the wide staircase. She viewed his study, a couple of guest-rooms, luxurious bathrooms and followed him down the corridor to the end door. He threw it open with a flourish. 'My bedroom.'

Their bodies touched as Rebecca went past him and her pulse increased considerably. She looked around. Trying to appear nonchalant, she saw it was a very large room with soft off-white carpeting, a huge bed that dominated everything, and floor-length windows that probably overlooked the garden at the back. The box-shape bed was covered in a heavy navy material with red-trimmings at the edges. There were a couple of impressive modern, but not too abstract, paintings on the walls, an antique chest-of-drawers in shiny honey tones, and a comfortable white wingback chair close to one of the windows. He must have a walk-in wardrobe, as there were no other cupboards or storage space to be seen. There was a lot of empty space; Becky mused you could turn a windmill on the floor without hitting any of the furniture.

She nodded silently and looked up at him; he was now leaning against the doorframe, arms crossed negligently and watching her. The breath caught in her throat when she saw the expression in his eyes. She understood why Lucinda Martin, or any other woman, would find him deliciously appealing. Once you knew him, he was a man to either hate or worship; and he was probably unscrupulous enough to take any woman if he made up his mind to do so. Raising fine arched eyebrows she swallowed hard and tried to warn herself about getting involved with him. 'You have a lovely home, Daniel. It's like something out of a glossy magazine.'

He shrugged. 'It suits me and my lifestyle.'

'Yes, I think it does. Did you choose everything yourself?'

'No, I just decided on the colours. A firm of interior decorators came up with the ideas. I didn't have time to get too involved personally, but I'm happy with the result.' He unfolded his arms and walked towards her.

Rebecca felt a slight panic rising from somewhere within her. She liked him, liked him too much for her own good, but if he thought that an invitation to the theatre automatically meant they'd end up together between his silken sheets, she was going to disappoint him. She turned deliberately and moved towards one of the paintings, pretending to give it a closer examination. To her mortification he'd clearly not intended to join her. He crossed the room without hesitation, to close one of the windows that had been slightly ajar.

She tried to silence her conscience for the wrong idea and she rushed into

151

haphazard sentences. 'If you took a tour of my flat, I'm sure you'd immediately feel hemmed in by its size, annoyed by the mixture of the various styles and items I've picked up through the years, and probably irritated by the colour schemes too.'

He came and stood in front of her. She could feel his breath on her face.

'What I saw of your flat, I liked. It was comfortable; it was a home. Your home is special because you created it . . . Just in the way you're special and unique! Sometimes I feel I'm living like a well-polished pea, in an empty pod. This house is not special — everything in it was chosen for me by other people.'

There was electricity between them. She could see the silver flecks in his eyes, the way the skin was tight over his cheekbones, and how his chin had the first faint signs of a beard. 'You're just flattering. There's certainly nothing special about me.'

As their eyes met and she was

mesmerised by the effect, she felt a shock run through her. She was sure that if she gave him the slightest invitation, he wouldn't think twice about inching her back until they were at the edge of that alluring bed. Had he asked her back to share more than a glass of wine in his living room? They were alone in his house and things could easily drift out of control. He was probably aware that he already had power over her, and most likely he could also tell she was wavering on the brink.

There was barely an obstacle left in the way before she lost her head and threw all caution to the wind even though she also knew it would be an adventure without any kind of promise.

She dithered and tried to ban thoughts of just letting things drift; her brain then whizzed along as her desire grew to let things take their course. She couldn't guess why he had singled her out, but she didn't really want to understand why. It seemed an eternity, but in reality it was only seconds before indecision began to take over again. What if this evening was all pre-planned; all just to put her in the right kind of mood to agree to anything he suggested?

Her throat was dry at the thought, and she pushed some escaping reddish-brown curls back from her ears. The idea that he was just looking for a meaningless affair sent a wave of apprehension through her and brought her back to earth with a thud. She looked down deliberately at her watch to break their eye contact. She shouldn't have come here this evening after all. He assumed his invitation included her unspoken consent to much more than a visit to the theatre. Who was she, after all? Just a temporary interest he had in someone living on the far edge of his life.

His world and hers had nothing in common. Her thoughts skidded and her apprehension grew. She didn't want a brief physical affair with someone who happened to be a leader of industry. Becky valued herself too much to ignore reality. She believed being in love with each other was a basic necessity for any real relationship, especially a physical one. Daniel noticed the change in the atmosphere. Rebecca turned slightly and moved towards the door. Still feeling slightly puzzled, he followed. She hurried down stairs again and walked back into the living room.

He went towards the music system; he began to ruffle through a shelf packed with CDs. Becky swallowed the lump in her throat with difficulty and she finally found her voice. 'Thank you for a lovely evening, Daniel. I think it's time for me to go. Would you get a taxi, please?'

He turned slowly to look at her and was clearly mystified by her sudden desire to leave. He studied her for a moment. 'Of course, if that's what you want.' Uncertainty was plastered across his face. 'Something wrong? You look like a ghost.'

'No . . . It's late. I'm tired — that's all.'

It wasn't easy to fool him. 'I don't believe you! What's wrong?'

Under his steady scrutiny it was hard to hang on to her intention of not falling so completely under his spell that her brain ceased to function. She speculated that the pursuit of a woman might be as exciting for him as chasing a deal, or buying a first edition at an auction. There was no other logical explanation why else was he spending time with someone like her.

Her thoughts unnerved her; made her wonder if she was just another trophy he intended to add to his collection. He might not venture into an off-hand relationship with someone like Lucinda Martin because they moved in the same circles all the time, but Rebecca Lomax was different. She was someone who'd drifted into his life and who'd provide him with a couple of nights or weeks of enjoyment without any commitment. He'd discard her as quickly as he'd entrapped her. Her thoughts circled, and the pleasure had gone out of the evening. She got up hurriedly and a tumble of confused thoughts and feelings assailed her as she did so.

His eyes widened at the look of almost panic. Searching for an explanation he demanded. 'Out with it, what's wrong? Did I say something to upset you?'

She was too busy with her own response to wonder what he'd think or how it would sound. She had to be truthful. 'I try to be honest, and I think it's time for me to go. I also think that it's not a good idea for us to meet again either.' The expression of surprise and confusion on his face made her hesitate, but by now her mind, and not her heart, was in control.

A shutter started to come down in his face, and his voice was irritated. 'Really? Why?' He stood stiffly and he eyed her with a chilled expression.

She recalled Ken's remarks about

157

'needing to let someone into her life if she wanted to be happy'. Her stomach knotted, and her colour heightened. 'Because I'm just wondering if you presume I'm prepared to drift into some kind of spontaneous affair. I'm not. And I don't believe in casual lovemaking either.'

His face was a mask. His voice held a slight note of sarcasm. 'You're jumping to conclusions. I promise you I had no intention of tricking you into a smudgy affair, or into my bed.' His eyes met hers disparagingly. 'I assure you I have never tried to persuade or trick any woman into sharing my company against their better judgment — until now it has never been necessary!'

She flinched; she was unwilling to face him and unable to turn away. 'Then I'm sure you won't be offended when I think it's very unusual for someone like you to show any special interest in some-one like me, unless there is an ulterior motive. We come from different worlds. My instincts just say there might be a hidden reason behind it all, perhaps an affair without any strings.'

With a voice edged with steel he replied. 'There is not, and never was, an ulterior motive. I enjoy your company, that's all. You say our worlds are different, but I don't think so, they're not different in a lot of ways. I've enough experience of people to judge, I assure you.' His lips thinned now with obvious anger. He viewed her with a sardonic expression and gave her a pseudo laugh, it raked through her. 'I won't try to persuade you to change your mind. I think the real reason is that you are scared, frightened of letting go. My father once told me that your parent's marriage ended in divorce, and I think that has coloured your attitude to men. My divorce damaged me, and your parents' divorce has affected you. Understandable and regrettable — because it prevents you from being objective. You think we men are all only interested in one thing, sex — but I assure you some of us consider other aspects of life are just as important. You told me once I was hypersensitive about my broken marriage — I think you are hypersensitive about men. As you feel threatened by my company you can be sure Miss Lomax that I won't bother you again in the future. Excuse me a moment! I'll phone for a taxi.' He went towards the door with rapid strides.

His voice sounded so callous that Rebecca wondered how she could ever have thought him to be kind. But she didn't have that thought for long. She knew there was truth behind what he'd said; she did find it hard to trust any man. It wasn't surprising that he felt angry. Nothing had happened; he'd made no move to compromise her in any way. Alarming thoughts raced through her mind. Suddenly she realised she could never dislike him at all, no matter what he said or how he acted. The truth was she loved Daniel Seymour. She loved him. Without realising what had gradually been happening she'd found a man she could

160

love for ever, and she'd pushed him away.

He attracted her physically; but all his positive and negative facets also fascinated her. Her jade eyes widened as she came to terms with her thoughts. It had nothing to do with logic and reason. Love was not logical; love was often irrational and nonsensical. She'd burned all her boats a moment ago and made it impossible for them to communicate on any kind of level again. She felt physically sick.

Given the chance, she'd turn back the clock, and throw caution to the wind. She'd have accepted him as he was — taken what he wanted to give — whether it was pure friendship or something more. Rebecca hadn't been looking, hadn't expected, to find a man who would govern her every thought like Daniel did. The signs had been there since she first met him. He'd succeeded in making her love him, and she'd destroyed any slight chance she might have had to be a part of his life.

161

With tears gathering at the back of her eyes, she followed him into the hall. She was unable to say anything. Grabbing her coat, she rushed outside to wait for the taxi on the rain-washed pavement. Later back in her flat she remembered she'd not thanked him for anything or said goodnight. When the taxi arrived, she'd thrown herself into the vehicle and given the driver her address in a choked voice.

9

During the next couple of days, Rebecca found there was a mindless solidity in her work that helped her to camouflage her mute wretchedness. Facing yet another evening alone at the flat, with thoughts of Daniel stinging at the back of her mind, Rebecca decided she needed to get away.

She could have arranged to go out with friends so that she'd stop thinking about Daniel for a while, but somehow she knew it wouldn't help — the facts wouldn't change even if she was part of a noisy crowd.

She knocked on Don's door and went in. He was sorting papers, his sleeves were rolled up to his elbows and his hair was completely dishevelled. He looked up. 'Becky! What can I do for you?'

'I'd like a couple of days off. I'd like

to go home to see my mother.'

He scratched his head and looked a bit surprised. 'Nothing wrong I hope?'

Rebecca shook her head. 'No. I just feel like it, that's all.'

'What's in the pipeline work-wise?'

'The text for Windthorpe contract, some more stuff for the washing powder people, the mock-up you wanted for Tony and Fay, and some other bits and pieces that are waiting.'

He rubbed his chin. 'If you can give me the mock-up by the week-end . . . the other things can wait a couple of days. How long do you want?'

'A long weekend? I can be back by Wednesday or Thursday if you need me. I'll try to finish all the outstanding work before I go.'

He eyed her and noticed the pale skin and listless eyes. 'Take a week. If you finish what's already in the offing, anything new can wait.'

★ ★ ★

164

The countryside sped by unnoticed. She wondered if a change of scenery and a visit to her mother would really help her to forget. Her gaze clouded over, and a lump formed in her throat. She held back gathering tears of disappointment as she thought about Daniel and what had happened. She'd only found out how much she wanted him when it was too late.

She took a deep breath. Luckily there was no one else sitting close by. She wondered how long she'd find herself in a dark tunnel, where there was nothing to look forward to apart from a second-class future.

At least it felt good to be back in her old bedroom and with her mother. Her room was the same as the day she left. There was even an old velour track suit in one of the drawers, and they still fitted. She skipped downstairs to join her Mum, making them tea in the kitchen.

Rebecca looked around. 'You've done it up since I was here last. It looks good. I like the colour; it's very cheerful.'

Her mother laughed softly. 'It was about time! The last time I decorated, you were still at university!' She gave Rebecca a mug. 'Just as you like it! A biscuit?'

Rebecca shook her head, and bent to stroke their cat that was winding its way in and out of her legs. It felt good to be missed and so welcome.

Her mother looked at her questioningly. 'Is everything all right love? You look a bit peaky.'

'Do I? Not enough fresh air and too much work I expect. How are things with you? Are you still helping Doris in the flower shop?'

'Yes. I enjoy it. Doris wants me to come in full-time.'

'Good! I'm glad you've found something you like doing. When we were small you just took anything that allowed you enough time to take care of us. You turned somersaults to make sure we were alright.' Rebecca paused.

166

'I appreciate what you did for us Mum, honestly! You made it possible for us to chose and go our own ways. You always put us first, we had what we needed, and we were safe and secure.'

Her mother's eyes shone. 'Oh, go on with you! It wasn't a sacrifice Becky. I'm proud of the two of you, and what you've achieved. I'm enjoying life again. I've recently joined a group that meets up every Tuesday evening, and we do all kinds of things together. Doris has tried hard to pair me off with Gordon.'

'Gordon?'

She nodded. 'He's a lovely man. I'd like you to meet him. His wife died of breast cancer two years ago, and someone brought him along one day; just like Doris took me. We get on very well.'

Rebecca tilted her head, and studied her carefully. 'Anything serious? I thought you'd never look at another man, after Dad.'

Mrs Lomax fiddled with the table-cloth. 'Not serious, just honest friendship.

Neither of us is looking for a partner, so it suits us fine to use each other as an alibi to stop being paired off with someone else.'

Becky was still surprised. 'I thought you'd never trust anyone else after Dad!'

'Becky, I'm human, and I often thought about finding someone else to love — but I never went looking. I told myself if I met someone it was fine, but if not it was also fine. Did I tell you that your father and his wife have split up, and he's waiting for divorce No.2 to come through?'

'Really? I'm not surprised. I expect it's easier the second-time around. You know we never tried to keep in touch with each other, apart from Christmas and birthday cards. Dad didn't find it hard to keep in touch with Neil. They went to football matches together, but he and I had nothing in common. Has he found someone else?'

A malicious grin overtook her mother's features. 'No, apparently she's dumped him and gone off with someone she met in work!'

Rebecca couldn't help laughing. 'Serve him right!'

'He phoned to tell me! I got the feeling he hoped I'd feel so sorry for him and he'd be able to stick his feet under the table here again. No chance, of course!'

'I should hope not. Not after all these years, and the way he treated you.'

Her mother shrugged. 'Stranger things have happened, but, quite simply, I just don't love him anymore. He killed those feelings when he packed his bags and left fifteen years ago.'

Rebecca sipped her tea. 'Do you think some women would have?'

'Taken him back? Probably! Some women ignore common sense.'

Becky's voice mirrored her own uncertainties. 'Love is a big gamble.'

Her mother looked at Rebecca speculatively. 'If we're lucky we find love once in a lifetime — with extraordinary luck, perhaps twice. It's worth hanging on to, however long it lasts. Even if marriage didn't work for me, I did love your father for quite a long time and I don't regret those years at all. We all want to love and be loved. I hope that you'll find someone one day. I was really sorry to hear you'd parted from Ken.'

Rebecca stirred her tea with a spoon in restless circles but didn't comment.

'Do you intend seeing Neil, now you're here?'

She came back to earth. 'Yes, I'll phone him later on. Perhaps he can come for a meal, if not I'll go and see him one evening.'

'He has a steady girlfriend now — Sharon. She's a lovely girl. I like her.'

'Wow! Then I've got to meet him, so that I can meet her!'

* * *

Rebecca looked at the title the artist had given the grey and brown painting on the wall opposite, and was more puzzled than ever. She shrugged and made room for someone else. She looked around to see Roger with some of the gratis champagne. The room was chock-a-block with art-critics, buyers, knowledgeable public, and people like herself; invited and without expertise.

She spotted the back of a head in the distance, the man reminded her of Daniel, her heart began to beat erratically and she had to tell herself not to be so idiotic. How ridiculous! It was only a spur of the moment but it made her pulse soar and her stomach plummet.

She began to fight her way through the crowd towards the lobby. She kept a look out for Roger on the way, in case he was on his way back to her. She wondered if he'd decide to wait for her near the bar. After they'd drunk a glass or two of champagne, they could safely leave; their work was done. Don's company had been involved with arranging the publicity for the exhibition; and seemingly it was all a resounding success.

The artist was still up-and-coming; one who had a rich patron who was prepared to support his career with the kind of money that made this evening possible. The artist's style didn't appeal to Rebecca much, but she noticed there were already a lot of 'Sold' tags on the paintings. Don was in Paris on holiday, and he'd asked Rebecca and Roger to cover for him on the night.

'Rebecca?'

She knew it was Daniel with her ears, before she located where he was with her eyes; he was straight ahead of her. Her eyes widened with surprise and she also immediately registered there was woman at his side. She could barely hide how delighted she was to see him, and she tried to ignore how her insides were swirling. Somehow she managed just to utter. 'Hello Daniel!'

Lucinda Martin looked at Rebecca speculatively, in surprise, and then directed her glance pointedly again at

Daniel; she was waiting for an introduction and it came. 'Lucinda, this is Rebecca. Rebecca Lomax, a friend of mine. Rebecca . . . Lucinda Martin.'

An unexpected surge of warmth surged through her. When she recalled their last meeting, there was no reason for him to be benevolent and call her a friend. Becky nodded at the other woman and received a barely discernable nod in exchange. 'I didn't realise you were interested in art,' said Daniel.

Unknown to him, his voice wakened buried longings. 'I'm not. My interest more or less starts with the Impressionists and ends in the twenties. Very conservative I'm afraid!'

As an added explanation she added. 'Our firm handled the PR for this exhibition, and Roger and I are here to represent Don — he's away.' When their eyes met, she felt a shock run through her. She was stunned by the thrill he still gave her despite the fact that he couldn't possibly like her anymore after the stupid way she'd acted. Rebecca glanced at Lucinda. She had a stiff expression on her beautiful face. 'As a matter of fact, I was on my way to find Roger, to make an exit. He went to get us some champagne ages ago.' She tried a stiff smile in Lucinda's direction.

'The drinks table is in the lobby, on the far side.'

She nodded gratefully. 'I'll try there then. Hope you enjoy the exhibition.'

Daniel glanced around. 'I doubt it; it's difficult to enjoy much in this crush.'

He didn't seem in a hurry, so she asked. 'Do . . . do you like modern art?'

'It all depends who the artist is, and what the painting is about. Mostly I think, your own instinct tells you if it suits your ideas or not.' He indicated with his chin towards the nearby paintings. 'Like any of them?'

Rebecca met his glance square on. 'No.'

He gave her an understanding smile. Lucinda was getting visibly impatient. She was fidgeting with her clutch-bag and clearly didn't like the fact that she was shut out of the conversation. They were interrupted by the appearance of Roger with half-empty glasses of champagne held up in the air above his head. 'Sorry Becky, I seem to have spilt half of it. Pity! I wanted to say 'Happy Birthday' in a fitting manner, but half a glass will have to do I'm afraid.' His words faded as he noticed the others.

Rebecca rescued one glass from his hand. 'You remember Mr Seymour, Roger? And this is Miss Lucinda Martin.'

'Yes . . . yes, of course.' Roger offered his hand politely and Daniel accepted it. Lucinda clutched her bag more tightly.

Daniel's attention wandered from Roger back to her, and he eyed her closely. 'Today's your birthday?'

Rebecca nodded and felt a little embarrassed. 'Yes.'

Polite as ever, he said. 'Congratulations and many happy returns of the day!'

'Thanks!' He didn't know it, but his words had made it a great day.

'Daniel darling, shall we move on? At this rate we won't see any of the paintings before we have to leave to meet the others.'

Rebecca didn't try to prolong the conversation. 'It was nice meeting you again Daniel. Please remember me to your parents, next time you see them.'

'Yes, I will.'

Lucinda tugged at his sleeve and left them, without more than a brief nod in Roger and Rebecca's direction. Daniel waited a moment before he moved away, his jaw tightening. He threaded his way through the crowd behind Lucinda and she hurried ahead into the crowd. Becky watched him until he turned a corner and was also lost to sight.

Roger hadn't forgotten. With a boyish grin he lifted his glass. 'Happy birthday, Becky! All the best and bottoms up!'

It was easy to smile. She'd just seen Daniel again, and he hadn't ignored her. 'Thanks! Perhaps we can grab another one of these on the way out?'

★   ★   ★

'Rebecca! Telephone!'

She hurried back from the copying machine in the corridor, threw herself in her chair and picked up the phone. 'Rebecca Lomax, can I help you?'

Daniel's slightly amused voice came down the line, and Rebecca smiled to herself as he spoke. 'Probably, but you work for someone else!'

'Daniel . . . ?' She searched her brain frantically to find a plausible reason for his phone call. Perhaps Don was applying for a new contract from Seymour that she didn't know about? He quickly stifled her curiosity,

'I wondered if you'd like to come out for a meal; a belated birthday present'

She listened with bewilderment and was lost for words. She hoped that her whirling emotions were suitably hidden away from her voice. 'But, I was so stupid and rude to you that Saturday evening at your . . . '

He replied impatiently. 'Let's not dwell on that, it's over and done with. There's no point in being in a huff with each other for the rest of our lives, is there? Like to come out for a meal with me or not?'

She sat back in her chair, momentarily floating in limbo; she found it was hard to formulate a sensible comment. A warm glow burgeoned inside and she felt buoyant and euphoric. 'Yes, I'd like to very much.'

'Good!' She heard the rustle of paper. 'I'll book a table at a small restaurant I know called 'Avec Plaisir!'. Ever heard of it?'

Swallowing the lump in her throat she said. 'No, I haven't.' She didn't care where they went, as long as she could be with him.

'I'll pick you up. Is this Saturday ok?'

Rebecca nodded at the telephone, and said. 'Yes.'

'Fine!' His voice sounded cheerful.

She could hear someone else in the background; someone within reach of his phone.

'If anything gets in the way, I'll give you plenty of warning. I'll see you Saturday, round about seven. I'll pick you up!'

'Yes, fine. Look forward to seeing you. Thanks for the invitation!'

'Bye!'

'Bye Daniel.' There was a click and the connection died.

She was elated, astonished, and a little shell-shocked. She warned herself not to let her fantasy jump too far ahead. Just to be back on good terms with Daniel was enough for the moment. She wasn't going to examine or calculate her actions, or any reactions in advance. She'd just follow her instincts, enjoy being with him, and let the future take care of itself. Her biggest immediate problem was what to wear. She picked up the abandoned papers from her desk, smothered the temptation to whoop out loud, and went back to her copying with a spring in her step.

Using an extended lunch hour to rush to some nearby shops, she reasoned she didn't have time to wander through all the big department stores. It was more likely that she'd find something in one of the small boutiques. They often had clothes you wouldn't find elsewhere; even if they were more expensive. An assistant came towards her when she entered the small boutique a stone's throw from the office.

'Can I help you?'

'I'm looking for a dress; elegant, not fussy, something special for an evening date, size twelve.'

The girl nodded and led her to a rack displaying dozens of dresses. 'Anything you think might be suitable here?'

Rebecca spontaneously picked out a couple, and the girl pointed her in the direction of the changing-room. She followed, carrying the chosen dresses on her arm.

Rebecca undressed hurriedly and

tried on a bronze-coloured dress that she'd liked on the hanger, but she found didn't fit. She knew that she'd a fairly good figure and the dress was marked in her size, but it was too small. The second one, in black fitted, but it did nothing for her complexion. She wanted something completely special.

The girl came back again. 'Everything ok?'

'Not really.' Rebecca was taking off the black dress. 'The ones I picked aren't what I want. Have you anything else you think might suit me?'

The girl tilted her head and eyed Rebecca carefully. 'I think I've something that will suit you down to a T.' Off she went.

Rebecca looked at the reflection in the mirror, and pulled her barely noticeable stomach in. The assistant returned a few moments later with a dress of a silk-like material. It shimmered in shades of green and black when moved. 'Try this! It looks sensational on. We only had three, all in different sizes, this is the last. The women who bought the others looked incredible in them.'

Rebecca took it and considered critically. It was short and tight, with a halter neckline and the straps crossed over at the back.

The assistant tried encouragement. 'Honestly, I promise it'll look great. A woman tried it on this morning and she looked really good in it, even though she didn't have nearly such a good figure. The only thing that stopped her buying it was the price. It's beautifully cut, and holds you in all the right places; although you're slim enough not to need extra support.'

Rebecca was sure it wouldn't fit. It looked too small when she held it in her hands. She slipped it over her head, pulled it down over her breasts, and then tugged it over her hips until the hemline came to rest just above her knees. Rebecca looked in the mirror and was amazed. It clung in all the right places and a panel of Lycra flattened her stomach completely. This time flat really was flat. The colour was also a perfect foil to the auburn tone of her hair. She never realised what good legs she had until now. She looked good — and felt good.

'Wow! It was made for you! You look great! Truly!' the assistant said.

Rebecca studied her reflection in the mirror. 'It's definitely a great fit.'

The assistant nodded enthusiastically. 'Perfect!' Another customer called for help and she hurried away, leaving Rebecca to consider in silence. She admired herself and then took it off and put her trouser suit on again. In her working clothes she looked dull after the vision of herself in the green dress. Rebecca looked at the price tag, and winced. She reasoned it was worth the money for the extra confidence it would give her, and more than anything else she wanted to look special for Daniel. She had no qualms to put down her credit card to pay for the most expensive dress she'd ever bought.

10

Her heart sank as she looked at the clock for the umpteenth time. There had to be a logical explanation why he was late — very late in fact — but what was it? It was nearly eight o'clock and she longed for the telephone to ring. Her mind wandered through all kinds of situations: a flat tyre or some other car trouble; an accident of some kind; an urgent business call?

She didn't like to think about the simple possibility that he never intended coming in the first place. That was just being silly; not someone of his stature! He was probably on his way, and there was a straightforward explanation.

Perhaps he was at the corner of the street at this moment? Her mind was a crazy mixture of hope and fear. The minutes ticked away and her stomach clenched tighter and tighter. If he was delayed, it only needed a phone-call from him to tell her so.

Usually, Saturday was the day when she caught up on the thousand-and-one things she had no time to do in the week. Today everything had centered on going out with Daniel. She'd been to the hairdresser this morning, had a makeshift lunch then a leisurely bath late this afternoon before finally manicuring her nails, dressing, and doing her make-up.

She was ready before time, and she'd renewed her lipstick once already. Time dragged and momentary panic turned into a real wave of apprehension that chilled her. She began to pace back and fore, nervously re-arranging things as she moved around the room. She clenched her nails until they marked her palms. At first the thought that he wasn't coming only loomed on the horizon like a fine mist, but then it started to cover her completely like a stifling blanket. She knew she hadn't made a mistake about the day or the

185

time — it had meant too much to her to muddle that up. She also remembered that he'd promised he'd warn her if anything prevented him coming. She felt ice spreading through her body and she threw her arms around herself in a gesture of self-protection. She began to wonder if he'd intended to date her for fun and had no intention of turning up. He might merely have wanted to get his own back for the way she'd rebuffed him a couple of weeks ago.

She glanced at her wrist-watch in a futile attempt to hold back time. It was twenty past nine. He wasn't coming. She gulped hard to try to stop them, but hot tears began to slip down her cheeks. Convulsive sobs shook her and she tried to control the disappointment. She fled into the bedroom and struggled out of the dress. Bundling it, she flung it in a heap into the wardrobe, and slammed the door. Standing in the bathroom she covered her features in cream and removed all traces of make-up; the face in the mirror was

186

white and icy fear twisted round her heart. She drew in a sharp breath.

Her stomach was clenched tight. She knew that she loved and wanted Daniel, but now it was clear just how desperately she'd wanted a chance to show him he was someone special in her life. Her breath solidified when she thought about the possibility that he had chosen to humiliate her in such a way. He'd always pretended how important honesty and truthfulness were, why hadn't he just ignored her and left things as they were if he didn't like her?

She was dumbstruck by his callousness and her own stupidity, but there was still an insatiable need for him crawling around inside her. Anger swept across the face in the mirror. She was angry with him, but even angrier with herself. She seethed with humiliation and made a resolution not to waste another thought on Daniel Seymour, he didn't deserve it. She slumped over and gripped the edge of the bath feeling slightly sick.

She put on an old track-suit, grabbed her keys and ran determinedly out of the flat, up the steps and began to pound the pavement — rounding the block several times trying to shake off the realisation he'd dumped her. She was still totally bewildered by his behaviour, but there was no logical explanation; he'd had plenty of time to send her his excuses by now, but he hadn't.

After a long and troubled night she found confused and tumbled emotions were her unwavering companion through the rest of the following day. She thought briefly about phoning him, or going round to his house to see him, but she decided it'd be juvenile and wide of the mark. She wasn't going to run after him. If he'd wanted to humiliate her, her appearance at his door would be the icing on the cake for him. She had a whole day of her own company to steady her thoughts, to sooth away some of the bitterness, and to put her life back on course. She tried to focus on the week ahead.

* * *

Becky buried herself in her work. Luckily there was plenty to keep her busy, and no one had time to notice that she was not as cheerful as usual. Don was vying for a contract for a well-known clothing company, and the whole office was involved. Demands for new versions of the various texts came by the hour, but for once she didn't mind — it kept her mind off other things.

She didn't care about working overtime either. By the time she got home every day, she was so tired it was all she could do to eat a makeshift meal and relax a little before she went to bed.

The pressure had eased by Thursday, and Don promised them all a few extra hours off on Friday afternoon. Rebecca was sorting out the mountain of paper on her desk when the phone rang.

'Rebecca Lomax.'

'Rebecca? Daniel . . . '

She drew in an audible breath and waited.

'I was wondering when I could make up for missing Saturday evening?'

She ripped out the words impatiently. 'As far as I'm concerned . . . never!'

His response was full of impatience. 'Rebecca, I'm suffering from jet-lag, I've a board meeting in ten minutes and I'm not in the mood to coax you!'

Her lips thinned. Who the devil did he think he was? 'Then I suggest you get some sleep, read what's on the agenda, and forget about me — in whatever order suits you best.'

There was silence, and Rebecca noticed her hands were shaking. She had to fight to control her swirling emotions.

His voice was aggressive. 'You're hopping mad? Didn't you get my note?'

Her breath burned in her throat and she reacted angrily. 'How many times have you used that pretext before? Perhaps it works among your society girlfriends, but not on me. It's Thursday, our date was last Saturday! It's taken you almost a week to phone? And then only to tell me you sent a note, one that was lost on the way?'

His voice was cold and bristling with indignation. 'It's the truth! I sent you a note with a package. I had to go away on Saturday. Don't you read the newspapers? The headlines would have told you why and where I was, even without my note. The gutter press pounced on the details like a bunch of starving hyenas.'

Rebecca heard his secretary in the background. Rebecca was struggling with coping with his voice, and the bottled-up anger of a week's annoyance; she was in no mood to try to repress her infuriation. 'I've been too busy to read newspapers . . . I've had other things to do. You're not the only person on this planet who is busy!'

'Oh, bloody hell!' His curt voice lashed at her. 'Look! I haven't time to argue over the telephone like this!'

'Good, neither have I!' Rebecca spat out the words contemptuously and flung the phone unceremoniously back into its holder onto the desk with a loud clatter. As the anger and resentment began to fade, she sat back in her chair, fingers tensely gripping the arms, until something inside her stirred uneasily. Her mind began to chew over what he'd said.

Unless she'd completely misjudged him, a warning signal told her something was wrong. Even if his way of handling people wasn't necessarily diplomatic, he was always straightforward and honest. Why should he make something up? And what did he mean about newspaper headlines? She got up quickly, pushed the hair off her face and went to look for Vera.

'Vera, do you have any back-copies of the newspaper? From Friday or Saturday perhaps?'

Vera shook her head. 'Sorry love. I read mine on the way here and usually throw it in the bin before I leave. I've still got today's; you're welcome to that.'

Rebecca shook her head absentmindedly.

Vera knew it was important; Rebecca wouldn't ask unless it was. 'Why not use the internet? I think some newspapers have editions online.'

Her eyes lit up. 'You're right! Thanks Vera!' Back at her desk she found newspaper websites. The Sunday editions already provided her with the answer.

'Body of Ex-Model discovered off the coast of Norfolk Island.'

'The body of ex-model June Moreland has been found in shallow water off the coast of Norfolk Island in Australia. Four years ago Miss Moreland, ex-wife of industrialist Daniel Seymour, was flying to a modelling assignment when a sudden storm drove the plane off course. It disappeared from the radar screens and radio contact failed. Amateur divers found the remains of the light-aircraft and the bodies of the model and the pilot this week.

'Identification after all this time is difficult, but Australian police are hopeful that Mr Seymour, who has volunteered to make the identification, will be able to recognise some items of jewellery that were found on the body, and that DNA tests will provide positive ID. Reliable sources report that Mr Seymour is already on his way.'

She stared unbelievingly at the words on the screen. He'd had a very real reason to cancel their Saturday date after all. He was on a plane to Australia already, otherwise the Sunday newspapers wouldn't have reported that he'd left. It didn't explain what had happened to the note he said he sent her, but now relief and remorse governed her thoughts. He hadn't deliberately ditched her after all.

At home that evening she continued to think how she'd misjudged him, how she'd accused him of lying. While pondering, she began the mindless task of rearranging her bookshelves. She barely noticed what she was doing, but it gave her hands something to do.

When the doorbell rang she flushed deep red in case it could be Daniel. She ran her hands through her hair and straightened the casual top she'd changed into after work. She drew a deep breath when she noticed a man's silhouette through the panel of milk glass in the upper part of her front door. She jerked it open and felt immediate disappointment when she found it was a uniformed delivery man with a parcel and letter in his hand. She signed for the items, and he whistled contentedly as he disappeared up the steps again.

Rebecca stared mesmerised at her address written in Daniel's bold hand-writing on both items. She closed the door, and just held them in her hands for a moment or so, before she slit the envelope and removed a single sheet of paper. It was dated late Saturday afternoon.

★ ★ ★

Dear Rebecca,

I've had to go away unexpectedly. They've found June's body. The Australian police want someone to identify the remains. June's sister asked me to do it because she's in hospital recovering from an operation, and won't be able to make a long journey for a while. Even though I no longer have any official responsibilities, I feel obliged to help, otherwise the official autopsy, and everything else, will delayed for months — or at least until her sister is fit enough to travel. Sorry I have to cancel our date this evening — especially at such short notice. I hope you'll understand and let me make up for it when I get back. I'll be in touch.

Daniel

She read the words and paled. She didn't know why the letter had taken so long to arrive — but it wasn't important. He had sent her a message.

She'd blamed him, and accused him. She picked up the package and turned it around several times before she broke the seal. She opened the cardboard box within. Tears misted her eyes as she undid the protective sheets and found *Pride & Prejudice*. There was a small card on top: *Happy Birthday — Daniel*.

Rebecca changed and called a taxi. When she was finally on the way to his house she thought about what she'd say to him. She wasn't even sure if he'd be at home, but the need to see him straight away and explain why she'd accused him, was greater than any fear that he might not ever want to see her again.

She paid off the taxi and felt a slight a moment of panic when she climbed the steps and rang the bell; her slender hands clutched the package with the books. The following minutes seemed like hours until she heard his footsteps in the hall-way. He opened the door and Rebecca noticed straight away he looked tired and drawn; probably from jet-lag.

He gave her a questioning look and his eyebrows lifted. 'Rebecca! What a surprise! I thought you'd firmly classified me with Dr Hannibal Lector, Captain Bligh, or Norman Bates in your list of popular people!' An expression that bordered on satisfaction glistened in his eyes, and he saw her obvious discomfort with smug delight.

'When you gave me the cold shoulder once, it scratched my ego a bit, but when I get the same kind of treatment nearly every time we meet it makes me wonder if I've just lost my touch, or if I'm going slightly crazy.'

She was humiliatingly conscious of his scrutiny. She bit her lip and shrugged to hide her confusion. Where could she begin? 'Daniel . . . I'm so sorry . . . I'

His grey eyes darkened but suddenly he moved out of the half-shadow and reached out for her in a single movement. The hovering smile she now saw in his eyes contained a sensuous flame. He pushed back a wayward strand of hair from her face and she felt his hand lift the hair from her neck. He looked at her for a moment and a prickle of excitement passed between them.

Her breath was uneven and her limbs felt unsteady as his arms opened wide. Rebecca didn't need a second invitation; she took a step towards him and was lost. His wonderful smile blossomed and his nearness made her senses spin; she felt like a breathless girl of eighteen. His mouth covered hers hungrily and his kiss sent the pit of her stomach into a wild swirl.

He exhaled a long sigh of contentment, and when he studied her face again, his eyes widened with a kind of false innocence. 'I thought this moment would never come.' His lips recaptured hers, and were more demanding. Rebecca was almost shocked by her eager response, but then she relaxed completely and enjoyed the sensation instead. Why hadn't she just realised from the moment she met him that he was the man she'd been looking for all her life?

Putting his arm around her waist he propelled her indoors and shut the door behind her with his foot. His hands moved gently down the length of her back and he pulled her into the shelter of his arms again.

'You're a very complicated woman, do you know that?' He said. 'I didn't think it'd be so difficult to convince you that we belong together. If I didn't love you so much, I'd have given up long ago.'

'I even tried to ignore you after the first time you came here. I thought I could control things, but I was only kidding myself.'

'You love me?' The words tripped over her tongue, and her mind tripped over the knowledge he'd actually admitted he loved her. She relished the thought for a brief moment and gave him an irresistible smile.

'Do you have a doubt about that? I can't remember when I had to work so hard to impress someone. It was like clambering up a slippery slope; one step forward, two steps back.'

They looked at each other and they exchanged a steady smile of happiness. 'And you?' She could tell he was waiting with baited breath.

It was a strange feeling to know she had power over Daniel Seymour. There was more than a spark of gaiety in her voice. 'Of course I love you. Why else am I here? I'm throwing myself shamelessly at you! I never thought anyone could ever make me hurl caution to the winds like this . . . '

She reached up and stroked the side of his cheek. ' . . . but you are such a special man. You mean more to me than anything else in my life Daniel. I never thought it would happen like this, but falling in love with you was so easy. It was only my uncertainty about whether you could really feel something for me that caused complications!'

He twisted his head, lifted her hand, and kissed the inside of the palm of her hand. His expression softened. Wordlessly, he dropped his arm across her shoulders and turned her towards the living room. She slipped an arm around his waist and relished the feeling of belonging, of coming home.

Suddenly remembering the reason she was here in the first place, she said. 'Thank you for the letter and the book; it was a wonderful idea — I can't accept it, of course!'

'It's my way of saying you mean more to me than anything in this world. I want you to know how much I love and trust you. I wouldn't have parted with it otherwise. From today on, it is yours!'

Rebecca felt quite euphoric. 'As ours, not mine! I've brought it back, because it belongs here.' She asked casually, although it wasn't really important any more. 'Why did your letter and the book only arrive today? Oh, by the way I'm so sorry I accused you of lying but I didn't know about June. We've been working like blazes this week and I haven't looked at a newspaper or seen the television for days. You left for Australia last Saturday didn't you?'

He had the grace to look uncomfortable. 'Ah!!' He led her to the sofa and then opened the wine. He looked a little sheepish. 'The delivery delay was my fault. When June's sister asked me to identify June, or what remains of her, I agreed. I guessed that formalities in Australia would take a couple of days and I went to the office to sign blank letterheads for emergencies, and gave my secretary last minute directions so that everything would carry on without me. I phoned you once or twice that afternoon about four, but there was no reply.'

Rebecca mused she'd been in the bathroom, with a loud radio.

'I didn't have time to keep on phoning so I wrote a letter and Irene packed the book for me. I told her to send them to you via special messenger. I knew that even though it was Saturday she'd get them delivered.'

He paused and grew quieter. 'I

thought . . . thought that I put them on Irene's desk on the way out, but I didn't. In the hectic rush I shoved them into the drawer of my desk with other papers and locked them away. Irene told me today she noticed I didn't mention the parcel again later on, but being the good secretary she is, she didn't question me. I only found them today — after we'd spoken this afternoon. I'm sorry!'

She lifted her eyebrows, tried to look annoyed, and failed. She couldn't be mad at him. Especially, now she knew that he'd tried. Her faultless executive was a human being after all. Her smile became a chuckle and he rewarded it with a resulting grin.

'I thought Irene would get the things to you on Saturday. I hoped you'd understand then that it was a special signal. I hoped we'd clear up all the confusion that evening. I went straight from the office to the airport. In Australia I focused on sorting things out as fast as I could. It wasn't a pleasant task. I'm glad they've found June's body. Even though we were divorced before her disappearance, she was part of my life.'

He handed her a long stemmed glass. 'I hope you don't mind me talking about her; I promise that you have no reason to be jealous of her, now or in the future. I was blinded by what she appeared to be and I didn't realise we were not compatible. We wanted completely different things from life. Until you came along, I'd more or less given up believing I'd find someone to love and respect. I'm damned lucky; I've found you. To us!'

Rebecca lifted her glass. 'To us!' She felt a warm glow and her heart sang. 'I'm not jealous. Why should I be? Perhaps I'm jealous of the time she had with you, but she must have been a stupid woman not to know your worth. In a way, the divorce left you free to restructure your life, and in the end you were free to love me!'

He took her glass and put it on the

table in front of them. Rebecca had no delusion about what sort of man he was. He liked to be in control, but she knew there was another side to his personality — he could be kind and indulgent. He also knew she was a woman with a strong streak of independence and would want a say in how their future should be; it didn't seem to bother him. He'd taken her heart with quiet assurance, because she wanted him to, and she revelled in the feeling of harmony they already had. Daniel was a strong man who she could rely on. He loved her; that was more than she had ever dared to hope. The future would bring what it brought. He lifted her chin with his finger and his lips were persuasive, and covered hers hungrily. 'I was intending to go to bed before you arrived, but now I've never felt more alive.' He looked her over seductively. 'But bed is still an attractive thought!'

Her flush deepened to crimson. There was a tingling in the pit of her stomach. 'Really?' Their eyes met; her heart turned over.

His nearness kindled feelings of fire.

He gathered her onto his lap. 'Umm! And when will you marry me?'

The breath caught in her throat. 'Marry you?' He smiled and her senses reeled as if she'd been short-circuited.

'That's the next logical move; it's where we're heading isn't it?'

'How can you be so sure? You don't know me really well yet! You don't know if we'll last. Lots of people fall in love, have a happy relationship, but don't necessarily get married.'

'That's true, but that's not what we both want is it? You're the other half of my soul. Somehow I always felt you didn't care a hoot about my job or my background. You love me and that gives my life real rhyme and reason. We're made for each other, although neither of us looked for commitment. I don't intend to possess you, or smother you.' He cleared his throat.

'By the way do you want children?'

Rebecca thought about having his

children, and nodded enthusiastically.

Inches away from her mouth, he smiled. 'Good! For the first time in my life I like the idea. I want you to myself for a while, but then it's up to you.' He kissed the tip of her nose, and then he satisfyingly kissed her soft mouth. She returned his kiss with reckless abandon. There was a smouldering flame in his eyes. He continued in a serious tone and watched her face. 'We've all the time in the world. I think it'd be an excellent idea to marry soon. It'll give us what we want; stability and happiness.'

Becky nodded with misted eyes. 'I'd want to go on working.'

'Fine! Why not! I'll always try to support you, whatever you want. We're going to disagree sometimes because we're both determined characters, but it takes one step forward to meet in the middle. I promise to always remember that.'

He did love her, it was written in his face. This was all she'd ever wanted.

We do hope that you have enjoyed reading this large print book.

Did you know that all of our titles are available for purchase?

We publish a wide range of high quality large print books including:
Romances, Mysteries, Classics
General Fiction
Non Fiction and Westerns

Special interest titles available in large print are:
The Little Oxford Dictionary
Music Book, Song Book
Hymn Book, Service Book

Also available from us courtesy of Oxford University Press:
Young Readers' Dictionary
(large print edition)
Young Readers' Thesaurus
(large print edition)

For further information or a free brochure, please contact us at:
Ulverscroft Large Print Books Ltd.,
The Green, Bradgate Road, Anstey,
Leicester, LE7 7FU, England.
Tel: (00 44) **0116 236 4325**
Fax: (00 44) **0116 234 0205**

FALLING LEAVES

Sheila Benton

When Richard employs Annie to update the computer system for his company, she finds herself, through circumstance, living in his house. Although they are attracted to each other, Richard's daughter, Katie, takes a dislike to her. Added to this, Annie suspects that Richard is in love with someone else, so she allows herself to be drawn to Steve, Richard's accountant. Annie feels she must choose between love and a career — how can the complications in her life be resolved . . . ?